FAREWELL,
MR. LOVELY

Also by Wendy Delaney

The Working Stiffs Mystery Series

Trudy, Madly, Deeply
Sex, Lies, and Snickerdoodles
There's Something About Marty
You Can't Go Gnome Again
Dogs, Lies, and Alibis
No Wedding For Old Men
Crazy, Stupid, Dead
A Kiwi Before Dying

FAREWELL, MR. LOVELY

A WORKING STIFFS MYSTERY
BOOK 9

Wendy Delaney

Sugarbaker Press

Sugarbaker Press
PO Box 1164
Boerne, TX 78006-1164

This is a work of fiction. Names, characters, places, and incidents are a product of the author's imagination. Locales and public names are sometimes used for atmospheric purposes. Any resemblance to actual people, living or dead, or to businesses, companies, events, institutions, or locales is completely coincidental.

Cover by Llewellen Designs

Printed in the United States of America

Farewell Mr. Lovely/Wendy Delaney – 1st edition, December 2023

ISBN: 978-0-9986597-7-0

For Kathy
Thank you for being you.

Acknowledgments

None of my books happen by themselves.

Farewell, Mr. Lovely started taking shape at an online plotting party attended by some of my wonderful readers. Not only was a crazy hour of fun, I came away with some terrific story suggestions. So, a big thank-you goes to my Duke's Cafe Facebook group members. Steve wasn't crazy about the idea that Marietta give him food poisoning at Thanksgiving, but I sure was!

Many thanks to fellow author, Kathy Coatney, for being my sounding board and the first set of eyes on my work. This writing gig wouldn't be nearly as enjoyable without you.

Elizabeth Flynn, sock diva and editor extraordinaire, you've helped me become a better writer. Bless you!

Thank you, Jeff, for supporting me on this grand adventure. Thanks for helping me breathe life into Steve, too.

Last but not least, I offer my heartfelt gratitude to my sharp-eyed dream team of beta-readers and supporters: Kathy Coatney, Heather Chargualaf, Brenda Randolph, Lori Dubiel, Jan Dobbins, Brandy Lanfair-Jones, Susan Cambra, Cindy Nelson, Denise Fluhr, Vicki Huskey, Amber Lassig, Christie Marks, Toni Mortensen, Beth Rosin, Donna Peterson, Diedre Herzog, Mattie Piela, Beth Carpenter, Kimber Mohr, Deb Tysick-Hawrylyshyn, Melissa Hogan, Annette Rouse, Melanie McCready, Mary-Jane Grandinetti Rader, Jenna Scully, and Jana Buxton.

Chapter One

"Your mother tried to kill me," Steve said, glaring at the steaming cup of peppermint tea I had waiting for him in his kitchen.

I wished I could do more to ease the discomfort of the man I loved. "I know it feels that way, but who was foolish enough to take a big helping of her mushroom risotto instead of my grandmother's stuffing?"

"Since I saw Barry chowing down on it, I assumed it was safe to eat because he made it. So, what was the culprit, the mushrooms?"

"From what I could get out of her when she called from the ER to see if we were okay, it was the rice."

Steve leaned against the white tile counter as if he needed the support after spending a sleepless night in his bathroom. "How the heck do you spoil rice?"

"By not refrigerating it when you cook it ahead of time. She meant well. Their fridge was full with the Thanksgiving turkey taking up a lot of space, and it never occurred to her that keeping the pan of rice on the counter all day could create a problem. At least not until she and Barry got sick in the middle of the night."

Grimacing as if he'd heard enough, Steve shook his head. "We're never eating there again."

Seeing how he and I were engaged to be married, and my actress mother kept inviting us over so that she could help us plan our wedding, I was okay with keeping our distance for a while.

Very okay.

I pushed the tea toward him. "Drink this. It will make you feel better."

My favorite cop looked at the steaming mug like he wanted to shoot it. "Sure."

"Okay, maybe it'll only make me feel better because I don't want you to get dehydrated."

"Fine." He took a sip and screwed up his nose. "What is this crap?"

"Peppermint herbal tea. I found it in your cupboard."

"Then it was left by my mother because she didn't like it any more than I do. I'll stick to water, thanks." He unscrewed the bottle he had out on the counter and gulped half of it down.

"Have you eaten anything today? I didn't want to take the time to pick up some food after I left the office, but I could run across the street to see if Gram has any broth or—"

"Your granny already came over with some cans of soup, but like I told her, I can't stomach the idea of thinking about food right now. In fact, I need to..." Muttering a curse, Steve rushed into the hallway bathroom.

"I am so sorry you're going through this," I called

after him. "But you're going to need to eat something eventually."

That didn't get me a response other than the groan I wasn't surprised to hear, considering what was going on in there.

Since he was otherwise occupied, I busied myself by searching his pantry, where I found two cans of tuna, a box of Cap'n Crunch cereal, a jar of pickles, and a sleeve of saltines.

As I grabbed the crackers to accompany the soup I hoped to coax Steve to eat, his cell phone started to ring.

"Is that my phone?" he asked between expletives.

I checked the caller ID and saw the name of Heather Beckett, his girlfriend back when we were all juniors in high school.

Now it was my turn to mutter an expletive. "Yes, but she can leave a message."

"She who?"

No one I wanted to talk about, although I was dying to find out why she was calling.

"Heather Beckett," I said as his phone finally fell silent.

"What does she want?"

Good question.

And I was still harboring just enough resentment about their relationship to be a little giddy with the fact that he didn't sound any happier to hear from her than I was.

Then his phone started ringing. It was Heather again.

"Do you want me to ask her?" I called out.

I didn't hear a "no" so I picked up his phone.

"Hi, Heather. It's Char. Steve can't come to the phone right now. Is there something I can help you with?" *And would you like to tell me why the heck you're calling my fiancé?*

Heather and I had been best buddies until the age of eleven, when I discovered I could do something my friends couldn't: tell when people were lying. And I made the mistake of gleefully calling her out during a game of Truth or Dare. She proceeded to label me as a freak in front of all our classmates and got us both called to the vice principal's office, where we were forced to shake hands and mend our differences like good little girls.

I had been sincerely sorry that I chose that night at Brandy Langerfeld's slumber party to show off at Heather's expense, and I had said as much.

Since Heather would only address me as "Freak" until we got into high school and she stopped talking to me altogether, it's safe to say my apology didn't take.

And I wasn't a bit surprised when I didn't hear anything but breathing.

Heavy breathing. Ragged breathing, as if she had run a mile to get to her phone.

Immediately, I sensed that the reason she hadn't responded had nothing to do with me. "Heather?"

"I really n-need Steve," she said, her voice choked with emotion.

"Sorry, but he's dealing with something else right now."

"It's an emergency!" she cried.

Now she wasn't the only one experiencing ragged breathing.

Trying to remain calm, I tightened my grip on Steve's phone. "A police emergency?"

"Yes! Please put—"

"You should call 911."

"I did! I'm not family, and the operator told me to wait for... Never mind. What am I telling you this for? I need Steve."

Then she should be less condescending about it. "Like I said, he's—"

"Don't make me come over there. Put him on the phone, *now!*"

I saw no reason to make Steve's miserable day worse by dealing with Heather up close and personal.

"Hold on." I rapped on the bathroom door just as Steve was flushing the toilet. "Sorry," I said, handing him his phone. "You'd better take this."

He glowered. "It couldn't wait two minutes?"

"Heather said it's an emergency." I skulked away from the door. "She wouldn't go into any detail, but something's wrong. Really wrong."

I wouldn't find out how right I was until Steve showed up on my doorstep five hours later with the news that Kevin Lovely was dead.

Chapter Two

Having spent the last two years working as an assistant to the prosecutor elected to also serve as coroner in rural Chimacam County, I knew the drill when it came to death investigations.

There would be an on-scene investigation conducted by one of the three senior prosecutors, who took turns as the coroner on call. Tonight, Ben Santiago, the head of the Criminal division, was the one who got called out to the Port Merritt, Washington, neighborhood where Kevin Lovely's car had crashed into a tree.

In Port Merritt, where Detective Steve Sixkiller served as a one-man forensic team for the fourteen-person police department, his analysis of the scene typically carried a lot of weight with my boss, Frankie Rickard, and all the department heads she had deputized.

From what little I was able to drag out of Steve, Ben had concurred with his conclusion based on the skid marks that Kevin Lovely's Camaro left a little over half a mile from his house.

"Single-car accident. The guy's kid saw it happen when he was out walking his dog. Said his dad was driving pretty fast, but I couldn't get much more out of him. He was pretty broken up," Steve said between spoonfuls of the canned soup I had heated up for him as if that were the end to the story.

Fozzie, the black chow mix occupying every square inch of the hardwood between our kitchen chairs, shot me a sidelong glance like he didn't believe it either.

"And?" I asked, watching Steve carefully.

"And what?"

Did I have to spell it out for him? "How come Heather was the one making the 911 call to report the accident?"

"She wasn't."

"She told me that she did."

He blew out a breath that signaled that this meal was going to come to an abrupt end if I kept asking questions. "Yes, she called 911, but the wife was the one to report the accident. That's when dispatch sent a unit and after the paramedics arrived on scene to pronounce the guy, they called me."

Wait. "Wife?"

"Yeah, wife, and they had two kids. Anything else you think you need to know so that we can stop talking about this?"

Yes!

"Lovely's not the most common name in the world." But it sounded so familiar to me.

Then I realized the reason why. "Holy smokes, is Kevin Lovely part of that interior design team that was working with my mother? You know, the 'dreamy one' she was so enthusiastic about."

Steve gave me a blank look.

Really? "You don't remember her saying that she pitched him the idea of doing one of those home improvement reality shows?"

He shrugged. "Maybe."

In other words, no. "You were sitting right next to me last night, when she went on and on about the Lovelys and how the two of them were naturals for TV."

"I may not have been hanging on her every word, but I can safely say that when I saw him, Kevin Lovely wasn't looking so dreamy."

"Well, my mom's gonna be disappointed when she hears the news. She was really impressed by that couple when they came out to discuss her kitchen makeover."

"Your mother lives in a new house. Nothing about it is begging for a makeover."

"You know Marietta. When she's not working, she gets bored and needs a project." And as long as that project had nothing to do with me, I was perfectly fine with it.

"Yeah." Steve pushed away from the table as if he were done eating as well as talking.

"Stay," I told my dog, who was angling closer to Steve's bowl as if there might be some leftover soup in his immediate future.

I locked gazes with Steve. "That goes for you, too, because I still don't understand why Heather called you all frantic about this guy. It's not like he was the current man in her life."

Steve cocked his head, his typical way of clueing me in without uttering a word.

"Oh. Who knew?" Then it hit me that he probably knew a lot more than he was letting on—as per usual. "Wait! Did you know about the two of them?"

"I wasn't keeping anything from you, if that's what you're asking," he said, carrying his bowl to the sink with Fozzie hot on his heels.

"They had to have been seeing one another for a while. How do you keep something like that quiet?" Because I hadn't heard a peep about them from any of my friends.

"If you'll recall, your friends didn't know about us for weeks."

"That was different. There was no husband or wife in the picture, so it wasn't like we *had* to sneak around so they wouldn't find out."

Stepping around the black fur ball that had been shadowing him since he arrived, Steve headed for the couch in the other room. "You're making a big assumption about them."

I wasted no time planting my butt onto the cushion next to him. "What do you know?"

"Nothing," he said, clicking on my flat screen with the remote.

I searched his face but didn't see so much as a flicker of deception. "It didn't sound like nothing."

"All I said is that you're making an assumption. We don't know anything about who knew what."

But I was pretty sure I could find someone who did.

✳

After he kept dozing off in front of the TV, Steve headed home around ten to get a solid eight hours without interruption from my alarm clock of a dog, who liked to wake me up bright and early for our morning jog. Or more correctly, just way too early on the Saturdays I wanted to sleep in.

But this wasn't one of those Saturdays.

And it wasn't the least bit bright. This Saturday morning was dark and gloomy with a heavy mist rolling up the hill toward Broward Park like a ghost in search of someone to spook.

The biting wind carrying that mist stung my cheeks and made my nose run, adding to the indignity I felt during my morning jog.

Because I wasn't running rain or shine for my health.

I had been hitting the streets, drippy nose and all each morning, because I could no longer fit into my wedding dress.

Which would have fit perfectly two months earlier if I hadn't cancelled our plans to get married at a Hawaiian beach resort. But after my wedding planner dropped the bombshell that my celebrity chef ex-husband and his supermodel fiancée had booked their ceremony for the Saturday before mine, I took it as a sign.

Okay, maybe it wasn't so much a sign as just a ridiculously cruel practical joke on the part of the universe. But I had wanted to run into Chris and meet his Danish bride, the gorgeous mother of their new baby, as much as I wanted to blind myself with tears this morning and run into a tree.

Which was going to happen if I didn't shut the floodgates. Again.

I wasn't even sure what had set me off this time.

Chris dumping me after seven years of marriage was the biggest favor he had ever done for me.

And I really didn't care that he had married the stunningly beautiful mother of his child.

Fine. I didn't care *that* much.

But did they really have to have their wedding at *my* resort a mere five days before Steve and I were to say our I-dos?

Since the universe's answer seemed to be, *Yes and get over it,* my response to that was to say no to the risk of running into one another at some random beach or restaurant on O'ahu.

After I had a good cry and told our families that the wedding was temporarily on hold, I started baking—my therapy of choice.

And now, eight weeks later, where was I?

Was I over it? Did I feel any less guilty for asking for my mother's help with covering the cancellation fees? Judging by the batch of chocolate chip cookies I baked after Steve left last night, not by a long shot.

Was this why I hadn't sat down with him to set another date for our wedding?

"It's been two months. What's your problem?" I shouted into the mist, slowing to a stop so that I could blow my leaky nose.

Fozzie looked up at me. It could have been my imagination or the tears clouding my vision, but I could have sworn his sweet brown eyes held sympathy.

Or it was simply pity because I could barely keep up with him.

"You've got it. That's my problem. You're more of an endurance runner than I am," I told my dog. "Plus, you haven't been eating as many cookies."

He woofed and went to water the base of one of the giant Douglas firs lining the entrance to Broward Park.

"Yep, I need to knock off the cookies." Along with the blueberry muffins I frequently treated myself to at my great-uncle Duke's diner.

But when I got there an hour later, I still found myself eyeing the yummy contents of the bakery case while I waited for Lucille Kressey, the queen bee of the local gossip circuit, to finish refilling the coffee cups of the customers at the counter.

"*Querida*," Hector Avocato called out from behind the grill. "You don't want anything in there."

Duke's weekend manager had been an advisor at a health club, where his mission had been to help people lose weight.

Given that the bacon and eggs I could smell Hector frying would be served dripping in artery-clogging grease, it seemed ironic for the kindly grandfather of six to give me any unsolicited dieting advice.

"Says you," I retorted, but he was exactly right. What I wanted wasn't sitting on display on a white paper doily. Although the cranberry cream cheese muffin sitting by its lonesome on the top glass shelf looked mighty tasty.

What I wanted this morning was information, and from the gleam in Lucille's light blue eyes as she closed in on me, she wanted the exact same thing.

"You heard the big news, right?" she asked, lowering her voice to a stage whisper.

I leaned in when she came to a stop at the other side of the bakery case. "About Kevin Lovely?"

Lucille shook her head, causing the points of the platinum bob framing her face to gently sway. "What a waste of good man flesh."

Not what I was expecting to hear from a woman more than old enough to be his mother, but I suspected that my mother would be quick to agree with her.

"So." Lucille inched closer. "Who do you think did it?"

What?

It was a car accident, so again, not what I had expected to hear.

"My money is on a woman." She arched her pale eyebrows. "From what I've heard over the years, the dude was quite the player."

Really.

"Come with me," I said, opening the kitchen door for Lucille. Because I needed to know what else she had heard.

Chapter Three

Sliding onto one of the wooden stools at the worktable in the center of the kitchen, I looked around to make sure that Lucille and I couldn't be overheard. "Okay, what makes you think that the guy was murdered?"

Lucille held up her hands as if I were pointing a gun at her. "All I know is that Mr. Love 'em and Leave 'em Lovely left a few broken hearts in his wake. And there's no telling what a jilted lover could do."

I doubted that a jilted lover forced the guy's car off the road. His son would have said something to Steve if he'd seen another car.

"Okay, so Kevin Lovely wasn't a paragon of virtue. I assume that his wife knew about these other women?"

"Hon, half the town knew, so I can't see her not being hip to him cheatin' on her."

Clearly, I had been living in the other half. "Do you know her?"

"Not well." Lucille smirked. "A burger joint isn't really her kind of place, if you know what I mean. I think Veronica Lovely is more of the tea room type, so our paths don't cross much. But ask anybody who went to the Lovelys to do their remodel, and I bet you'd always hear the same thing. How Veronica Lovely has an eye for this stuff. How she can take an old, tired room and transform it into a thing of beauty. Just like one of those gals on a home improvement show. She's got it up here." Lucille tapped her temple. "And then her husband was the guy with the know-how to turn her vision into a reality."

No wonder Marietta had been pitching them the idea of a reality TV show.

"They made a good team." Lucille tsked. "Can't imagine that a smart lady like Veronica would've wanted to off the dude."

That seemed unlikely to me, too, especially since I already knew from Steve that the "dude" offed himself in a car accident.

"I mean, they're *it*—the dream team when it comes to updating some of these old Victorians in town. Why, just last week, I heard someone say that they wouldn't be able to start on her remodel until March. They're that busy." Lucille stared across the table at me. "So, even though her husband was two-timin' her—most recently with Heather Beckett. You knew about that, right?"

I nodded. I didn't dare mention exactly how I knew if I didn't want my name linked with Heather's when every salacious detail about her relationship with Kevin Lovely started hitting the gossip circuit.

"Well, you just don't kill off half of the dream team. It's bad for business."

"I'm sure you're right."

Lucille pressed closer. "That's why I think it was one of the chickadees who got dumped."

"Or it was just a car accident."

"I take it that's what Steve told you."

"Uh…" I wasn't about to let her quote me as her news source. "I'm just making an educated guess based on how car crashes usually happen around here."

She scowled. "Sure you are. You're not the only one around here who can tell when someone's lyin'."

"Moi? I'm just stating the obvious," I said a split second before Hector called to Lucille that one of her orders was up.

"What's obvious is that this was no accident." She pushed away from the table. "Mark my words, it's only a matter of time before someone at your office agrees with me."

I didn't have the heart to tell her that Ben Santiago had already completed his investigation and would no doubt cite "Traffic accident" as the manner of death on his report.

"Hey," I said as Lucille headed toward the door in her squeaky orthopedic shoes. "Do you happen to know how long Heather and Kevin Lovely had been seeing one another?"

Lucille squeaked to a stop with a pleased curl to her tangerine-painted lips. "You don't?"

"We're not exactly besties." As she well knew. "So no."

"Rumor has it they've been goin' hot and heavy ever since the dude did some work at her house last summer.

According to Miriam, that old muscle car of his was parked down the street from Heather's at all hours of the night. Like parking it half a block away was gonna keep the neighbors from suspectin' anything."

Especially with a neighbor like Miriam, a Duke's regular who was one of Lucille's best sources of gossip.

"Not to interrupt or anything, but your order is up!" Hector pointed his spatula at Lucille. "As in *now*."

"I'm coming. Sheesh, hold your donkeys," Lucille said, waving him off while she waited for me to catch up with her. "Why'd you want to know about Heather and him? You think she's involved in his death somehow?"

I was more curious about how involved she had been in his life. "No, I was just wondering."

"Yeah, I don't consider her to be a serious suspect either, although I can't help but wonder if he was on his way to see her when he got run off the road."

She probably had that half-right, but I kept my mouth shut and shrugged.

Lucille scowled. "I have a feeling that you know a lot more than you're sayin'."

"And I have a feeling that Hector's going to chase me out of here with that spatula if you don't get your butt in gear and pick up that order."

"Yup, you definitely know something."

"Trust me, it's not much because I haven't talked to Heather in months." Not counting last night.

"I didn't hear a no, so until someone tells me otherwise, that's gonna be my theory. That Kevin Lovely had a hot date with his latest girlfriend and some prior paramour forced his car off the road."

As Lucille's wacky theories typically went, this wasn't outlandishly wacky. It was just unsupported by Steve and Ben's investigations.

"Of course, Miriam thinks it was the wife," Lucille added, slanting me a glance.

"So she doesn't agree with you about how that would be bad for business."

"She saw Veronica do a couple of drive-bys in the neighborhood, so Miriam has a theory of her own."

If Steve hadn't already told me about the Lovelys' son witnessing the accident, I would have taken this information to Ben first thing Monday with the hope that he'd ask me to get a statement from the wife as well as the son. Maybe a statement from Miriam, too.

But there was nothing about Kevin Lovely's death that Steve had found suspicious. He'd made that abundantly clear.

And I was quite sure that Ben wouldn't be interested to hear that Gossip Central was trying to turn this single-car accident into some sort of revenge murder.

Still, the fact that Kevin Lovely was having an affair that his wife knew about felt like information that someone should provide to Ben before he signed off on his investigation.

I just didn't know if that someone should be me.

Chapter Four

After I left Duke's, I headed over to my grandmother's house to see if she wanted to join me for some post-Thanksgiving Day sales shopping in Seattle.

I needed the distraction from the hamster wheel my brain had been racing on ever since I answered Steve's phone and spoke to the "other woman" in Veronica Lovely's life—the one she apparently was fully aware of.

And unfortunately for me, the one who was stepping out of the blue Prius parked across the street in front of Steve's house.

"Swell," I grumbled as I turned into my grandmother's driveway.

I had barely cracked open my car door when Heather rushed it like one of my mother's fans seeking her autograph. "Do you know where Steve is?"

"He might still be at work." He had texted me an hour earlier that he had completed his report, but that he and a buddy were going to grab a burger and watch the game. In other words, Steve needed some downtime, and I shouldn't expect to see him until dinner tonight.

"I called him at work. I called his cell, too, but it went to voicemail."

Probably because he didn't want to talk to her. Which gave me a teensy bit of satisfaction. It would have felt even better if Heather hadn't shown up looking like a zombie extra from one of my mother's teen scream movies.

I had a feeling that a torrent of fresh tears might flood from Heather's bloodshot blue eyes if I didn't provide her some crumb of hope in the next few seconds, so I opted for kindness instead of honesty. "I'm sure he'll call you back when he has a free minute."

Maybe at halftime.

She wiped away the teardrop trickling down her pale cheek. "I think he's avoiding me."

That would be a safe bet. "I'm sure he's just busy. You know, wrapping up the investigation."

"When I talked to him a couple of hours ago, he told me there wasn't anything else to do."

Then I didn't know what to tell her. "I'm sorry. I don't know when he's going to be back." *So please go home.*

Heaving a sigh, Heather looked up and down the street as if she needed some visual confirmation that Steve wouldn't be coming to her emotional rescue anytime soon.

"But I'll tell him you stopped by." I stepped away from my car with the hope that she'd do the same.

Her feet didn't budge. Instead, her mouth drew into a grim line. "Yeah, that'll help."

"Sorry," I said without feeling the least bit apologetic

considering all the crap I had taken from her over the last twenty-five years. "That's the best I can do."

Heather pulled her black hoodie tight as if the misty breeze stirring the leaves at our feet were an Arctic blast cutting through her slender frame. "That's pretty much all I've heard since last night. No one will talk to me."

And I saw no reason why I should be any different.

This was a conversation she should be having with Steve. Not that I wanted the two of them to spend any more time together than was absolutely necessary, but considering what she wanted to talk about, better him than me.

Narrowing her puffy eyes, she gave me a hard stare. "He told you what happened, right?"

The last thing Steve would want was me discussing his case with anyone, so I knew I had better stick to the minimal level of information that would have made it to Duke's Cafe. Minus the juicy bits of gossip Lucille had supplied. "I heard about the accident."

Heather shook her head so vehemently that her toffee-blond ponytail escaped from under the hood that had been covering it. "Then you heard wrong, because this was no accident."

Surely, Steve would have told her that much when he spoke with her earlier. "But—"

"I know that Steve doesn't want to hear it, but there's no way that this was just a car accident. She's behind this somehow."

"She who?" A former girlfriend like Lucille suspected?

Heather choked back a sob. "His wife."

No wonder Steve didn't want to hear it. Still, if she had witnessed Veronica Lovely making a threat against her husband, Heather needed to bring that information to Steve or Ben to give them a good reason to continue with their investigations.

If it was just her broken heart in search of someone to blame for Kevin Lovely's death, then case closed, or it soon would be after someone took Heather's witness statement.

Again, I didn't know if that someone should be me. But since Steve and Ben weren't around and Heather was, I didn't see the harm in handling the preliminaries. Then I'd know, for sure, how seriously to take Heather's accusation.

"Do you want to come in? I can make some coffee and we can talk." Never mind that Heather Carver Beckett had been my nemesis since sixth grade, and she was the last person I thought I would be sitting down with for a heart-to-heart.

She blinked as if she hadn't heard me right.

I couldn't blame her. I barely comprehended the words that had just come out of my mouth.

"I don't…" Her brow furrowed. "You don't have to—"

"I know. It's just coffee."

"Right," Heather muttered.

But as we headed toward the house, she and I both knew that this was going to be a lot more than coffee.

It was going to be weird.

*

"Want to tell me why Heather Carver is sitting in my dining room?" Gram whispered as I willed her ancient coffeemaker to hurry up and complete its brew cycle.

"Heather Beckett. She hasn't used her maiden name for years."

"Whatever. That girl hasn't been inside this house for a lot longer than that, so why is she here now?" Gram gave me a long look over her silver-framed trifocals. "Last I heard, you two were barely speaking."

"I know, but that was before the guy she's been seeing was killed." I left out the part about the guy being married. There was already such an undercurrent of tension in the house I could almost hear it crackling. I didn't need to add any shock value.

Gram sucked in a breath. "Kevin Lovely?"

Was I the only one who hadn't known about their affair?

I shushed her as I reached into the cabinet for two coffee mugs. "He had some sort of car accident last night."

"How horrible for his family and, of course, everyone else involved."

I assumed she was referencing Heather with that last part.

"Oh, speaking of which…" Gram turned to me. "Do you think your mother knows?"

"I doubt it." This was the kind of news that Marietta would react to, and since I hadn't heard a peep out of her since she called yesterday morning, it was safe to assume that she was in the dark about the death of her would-be reality TV star. And that was fine by me. I was already dealing with as much reality as I could handle.

Gram inched closer, her voice solemn. "Someone should tell her."

This time I was quite certain that someone should not be me.

"I'm a little busy with Heather at the moment," I said, holding the steaming carafe to emphasize the point that my hands were full.

"Doing what, exactly? Given all the water under the bridge with you two, I wouldn't think yours would be a shoulder she'd want to cry on."

As per usual, the woman who raised me was absolutely right. I was quite sure Heather didn't want to make any physical contact with me. Sitting across from one another at a table was probably the closest either one of us wanted to get. At least it would provide me a good vantage point to read her body language.

I kept my voice low as I poured. "She just needs someone to talk to, and Steve's not available. It was just a coincidence that I happened to be here."

"I take it Stevie's the one who gave her the bad news?"

Placing the mugs on a serving tray, I nodded. "Last night, after he left the scene. He knew that they were *involved* so he did that as a courtesy." Plus, she would have kept calling if that courtesy hadn't been extended.

"That's what we need to do," Gram said, adding the

cream and sugar set she reserved for company to the tray.

"What?"

"Make a visit to your mother as a courtesy."

I splashed some milk into the creamer. "Wouldn't you rather go to the city and shop the after-Thanksgiving Day sales? I shouldn't need more than an hour with Heather." Especially if we kept the awkward silences to a minimum. "Then we could catch the one-thirty ferry to Seattle."

Gram gave me the *look*. "We have to tell her. It's the right thing to do."

Heaving a sigh, I added a couple of spoons to the tray. "Fine."

"I made a pot of chicken soup yesterday that I wanted to take over to your mom, so this is good timing."

It didn't sound so good to me. "Uh-huh."

Gram pulled out two butter-yellow cloth napkins she had embroidered long ago with orange pumpkins and set them next to the spoons. "Do you think Heather would like some soup?"

"I think she just wants the coffee."

"How about some pumpkin spice muffins to go with it? I bet she hasn't eaten all day."

Gram was making me increasingly nervous with her hovering, and when I was nervous I needed something to munch on. So despite my determination to avoid all things muffin today, I caved. "That would be great," I said, picking up the tray. "Thanks."

Gram gave my back a pat of encouragement as if I

needed it more than the muffin. And maybe I did because I wasn't at all sure what I was getting myself into.

"Sorry to keep you waiting," I said to Heather when I joined her in the dining room.

Her full lips stretched into a half-hearted smile, something I'd become accustomed to seeing with Heather when she had to acknowledge my presence. But today I cut her some slack because it was probably the best that she could do.

Setting the serving tray in the center of the white lace-covered table, I splashed some milk into one of the coffee mugs, took a spoon and a napkin, and then settled into the hardback chair opposite Heather. "Please help yourself."

As Heather spooned some sugar into the other coffee mug, Gram set two of her good china plates on the table along with a platter of four muffins.

"Is there anything else you girls need?" Gram asked like the good hostess I knew she was trying to be.

While Heather stared into the depths of the steaming mug in front of her, I turned to my grandmother. "I think we just need a little time." *And privacy.*

Gram nodded. "I'll leave you to it then."

I reached for a muffin and hoped that Heather would do the same. I knew that I shouldn't care what the perfectly toned creature across from me thought about me eating a few hundred calories of fat-laden carbs in front of her. But I did, and when the only movement she made was to sip her coffee, I set the muffin down on my plate.

Dousing my frustration with a gulp of coffee, I racked

my brain for something to say that would get Heather talking.

"You don't have to try so hard, you know," she said, gazing at me over the rim of her mug.

I nearly choked. "I—"

"I couldn't help but hear what your grandmother said in there."

Oops.

"And she's right. There's a lot of water under the bridge with us." Heather shook her head as if she were shaking off some of the memories we shared. "Most of it probably my fault."

Probably? The best friend of my youth was being kind to herself, but since this was as close as I thought I'd ever get to an apology, I kept my mouth shut.

She wrapped her hands around her mug. "But I appreciate this...this effort so that we can get past all that."

Okay, now she was making me feel guilty about inviting her inside so that I could hear more about Kevin Lovely's wife. "It's not a big deal. Just coffee." And a muffin that Heather hadn't given so much as a cursory glance to.

Dang it.

"I'm wasting my time here, aren't I," she said after several seconds ticked by in silence.

I wasn't sure how to respond to the ache in her voice. "What do you mean?"

"Steve's done as much as he can do. That's why he's avoiding me."

Absolutely right. "I really don't know, I'm sorry. He

only told me that he had plans for this afternoon."

"Those plans should include talking to Veronica Lovely." Heather took an angry swipe at the tear spilling over her mascara-free lashes. "But I bet they don't. He made it pretty clear that he didn't want to hear what I had to say about her."

"I'm sure that he did a thorough investigation of the accident scene and—"

"I told you. His death was no accident."

"I know it feels that way."

"You don't get it," Heather insisted. "Kevin called around four-twenty to let me know that he was leaving his house early. Veronica had made a scene about him missing another dinner with the kids, and he wanted to get out of there before it escalated."

That didn't sound particularly suspicious to me. "Okay."

Heather huffed an impatient breath. "And then just as he was leaving, she must've done something to try to stop him. It had to have been like that. He knows that road. He's lived there for years! No, she caused this. I'm certain of it."

I could understand Heather wanting to find someone to blame for the death of her boyfriend, but I had yet to hear anything that truly implicated Veronica Lovely.

"Just because she wasn't happy that her husband was heading over to see you doesn't mean—"

"I know that!" Heather snapped. "I'm not talking about where Kevin was going. It's when he left."

Failing to see her point, I shrugged.

"Right after he called me! But Veronica didn't call 911 until almost six!"

"You don't know that." And I couldn't imagine anyone working dispatch last night divulging that information to her.

"That's when the 911 operator called Steve," Heather insisted with greater volume. "My grandfather clock was chiming the hour when he stepped through the door, so I actually do know that."

"Then you also know that he would've talked to her last night, so there's really no need—"

"Yes there is, because I'm sure she lied about everything that happened after Kevin called me. And if someone doesn't talk to her again, she's going to get away with this. In fact, I think that someone should be you."

Chapter Five

"You're being awfully quiet," Gram said as I drove up the hill to Marietta's house. "I'm pretty sure you haven't uttered more than two words since you had your chat with Heather. Should I assume that it didn't go very well?"

"It went fine." In a weird, alternate universe kind of way.

Gram leaned back in the passenger seat of my Subaru. "It still seems very strange that she'd want to talk to you of all people."

Tell me about it. "Yeah, I know."

"Did she think you'd have some inside information about the investigation into her *friend's* death?"

"No, like I said, she just needed to talk to someone and Steve wasn't around."

"Uh-huh. Something tells me that's not all that girl wanted."

I pulled into my mother's driveway and killed the ignition. "She also might have wanted to apologize." In a roundabout way. Which showed how desperate Heather was to recruit me as an ally.

"Really!" Gram said. "I never thought I'd live to see that day."

"It's not a big deal." And I didn't want her to turn it into one with more probing questions, so I directed her attention to our task at hand. "I'll get the soup. It's only a little after one, so why don't you let me do the talking in there. I'll deliver the bad news as gently as I can, and then you should say something about us needing to leave. If we don't hit any traffic, we'll be able to make the ferry with minutes to spare."

Gram yanked the plastic container of soup from my hands. "Charmaine Digby, I raised you better than that. This news is going to upset your mother, so plan on staying for as long as it takes. Grab the shopping bag from the back seat. I put the muffins you girls didn't eat in there along with some cookies. Some cheese and crackers, too. I wasn't sure what your mother would have on hand."

I came from a long line of women who ate in times of crisis. Kevin Lovely's death shouldn't register more than a blip on my mother's crisis meter, but if she needed a muffin and a cookie or two to get through this day, I was all for it. Especially since that was exactly what I now needed.

I followed Gram to the front door, where she knocked and then immediately used her key to let herself in. "Yoo-hoo, anybody home?"

"Hello, hello!" Marietta called out, descending her staircase in a thigh-length crimson kimono over shiny black satin pajamas. "What brings you girls over at this hour of the morning?"

Any time before two in the afternoon was morning to my mother since she typically slept until noon on the days she wasn't needed on a set. But she wore a shade of red lipstick that matched her kimono, there was an artful flush to the apple of her cheeks, and her kohl-lined green eyes looked clear and bright, so she'd obviously been up for a while.

"We wanted to see how you and Barry were doing." Gram held out the container of chicken soup in her hands as if it were an offering to the barefoot goddess approaching us. "If you were still under the weather, I brought soup."

"Thank you, Mama," Marietta said. "That was very nice of you."

"And some other goodies," I added as my mother eyed the bag dangling from my arm.

She winked at me. "Very, very nice."

Taking the plastic container from her mother, Marietta led the way into the immaculate gourmet chef's kitchen she thought needed upgrading. "I do appreciate all this, but we're feeling much better now. So much so that Barry got up early to catch a ferry and spend the day with his son."

At least one of us made it into Seattle today.

"Oh, good." Gram stepped to the kitchen table and peered out the window, where gray, puffy clouds gathered. "We seem to be between rain showers right now, so hopefully the weather will cooperate the rest of the day for them."

"I hope so." Marietta released a peevish sigh. "We need a break from the rain and the constant overcast. Day after day of it can get so depressing."

If she thought a little bit of drizzle was depressing, wait until she heard about Kevin Lovely's accident.

Gram shot me a pointed look of warning, giving me the none-too-subtle cue to ease into that discussion by serving up an appetizer course of chit-chat.

For that I required some fortification.

"Are you hungry?" I set the shopping bag on the granite countertop of the center island and started unloading it. "We have muffins."

"Ooh, those look good," Marietta said, leaning over to take a sniff. "Smell good, too. I assume you made them."

Since I was a former pastry chef and enjoyed baking for the family, it was a safe assumption. "Not this time. Gram did the honors. Why don't you join her at the table and I'll get us some coffee."

Not that I needed more caffeine in my system, but if I wanted the next few minutes to go well, I needed it to feel as normal as possible.

Beaming, my mother wrapped her arms around me. "How fun. Instead of spending this gloomy day alone, I'm having brunch with my favorite girls."

While smothering me with her jasmine-scented embrace, she lowered her hands to the roll spilling over the increasingly snug waistband of my blue jeans. When she pulled back, Marietta said nothing about the flabby midsection she had just frisked.

That was some consolation. Until her collagen-enhanced lips curled into a sad smile.

Are you trying to sabotage your wedding by not being able to fit into your dress?

It was the same question I asked myself every time I went to the store for a head of lettuce and came home with a pint of mocha almond fudge. And every time I convinced myself that my need to self-medicate with that pint of edible relief had nothing to do with the wedding I had yet to reschedule.

Okay, almost convince myself.

"How's Steve doing?" Marietta asked, following me to the appliance garage where she stowed her coffeemaker along with a premium selection of single-serve pods.

"He's fine." Pulling three tall glass mugs from an overhead cabinet, I hoped she was inquiring about how he was feeling after his bout of food poisoning and not laying the groundwork for more in-depth questions.

She nudged closer. "So everything's back to normal?"

If you considered everything that had occurred since the moment he received that call from Heather normal. "Pretty much."

"Great." Marietta plucked three pods of Italian roast from a storage rack and set them in front of the brewer. "You know, when the two of you were here with the family for Thanksgiving, I really thought you might have some news for us."

"No news." At least not the wedding date news I knew she had wanted to hear.

I popped a pod into her coffeemaker and while it

whirred to life, I set all the muffins and cookies on a plate and handed it to my mother. "Want to take this to the table and have a seat? I'll bring our coffee over."

Marietta set the plate on the island behind her. "Not just yet."

Dang.

Her eyes held a predatory gleam as they locked onto mine. "When do you think you'll have some news for us?"

"Actually, there is something—"

"You've finally set a date!" she squealed, turning to her mother. "I told you they'd make an announcement during the holidays."

Gram patted the seat of the chair next to her. "Sweetheart, that's not the news we're here to give you."

"I don't understand." A second later, Marietta sharply inhaled. "You're sick. Oh, Mama!"

"No, no. I'm fine." Gram patted the chair again. "Please sit down."

"If you're fine and Steve's fine..." My mother blinked back tears as she whipped around to me. "Please don't tell me that you've been holding back on the reason you haven't set a date. I couldn't bear it if—"

"Our news has nothing to do with me or the wedding!" I blurted out to keep her from jumping to any more conclusions. "Kevin Lovely is dead."

Chapter Six

"Oh, this is horrible. Poor Veronica. To lose her husband *and* her partner this way." Marietta pushed aside her coffee cup and grabbed her cell phone. "I'd better let my agent know that we're going to have to scrap the show idea. I had such a cute title for it too—*A Lovely Makeover.*"

Gram swatted the phone out of her daughter's hand. "That's what you care most about at a time like this? Shame on you."

"No, of course not. I feel Kevin's passing as much as anyone who knew him. He was such a lovely man." Color flooded into my mother's cheeks as she realized what she had just said. "No pun intended. I'm just saying that the camera would have loved him. And as a couple, the Lovelys were so engaging. The way they bounced ideas off one another, so collaborative while at the same time very individual in their taste and sensibilities. Really, the yin to the other's yang. Their banter alone could have made them stars of one of the more popular home improvement shows on the air."

Clearly, Marietta hadn't been aware that the Lovelys' marriage was in trouble.

She heaved a sigh. "Now we'll never know."

Gram patted the hand she'd swatted a minute earlier. "Maybe it's just as well."

Straightening in her seat, Marietta withdrew her hand. "What? You don't think I could've pulled some strings to get those two a meeting with a production company? I still have some clout, you know."

Now it was Gram's turn to sigh. "I wasn't suggesting that you didn't. It's just that your *lovely* man might have been engaging in some extracurricular activities that wouldn't have made for great TV."

"What are you saying?" Marietta asked her mother.

Gram pointed at me just as I was about to bite into a muffin. "You tell her. You know more about this than I do."

Which was based upon gossip and unsubstantiated suspicions, most of which I didn't feel right about repeating.

I reluctantly dropped the muffin onto my plate. "Pretty much all I know is that Kevin Lovely had been cheating on his wife, and according to the rumors floating around town, this wasn't the first time."

My mother's eyes widened. "Really? I didn't sense any trouble between them when they came to the house last week. In fact, they were rather cute together."

Then she hadn't been the only one with some acting ability at that meeting. "I think their professional relationship was still working, but I have it on pretty good authority that there were problems at home."

To say the least.

"Maybe that explains it," Marietta said, staring out the window.

Gram leaned in. "Explains what, honey?"

"Why Kevin acted a little cool when I pitched the idea of the show. I passed it off as natural reticence to put their business under such a bright spotlight, but maybe it wasn't the business he was concerned about."

"Not everyone wants to be in the spotlight," Gram said between sips of coffee. "It could also be as simple as that."

"True, but I think they recognized how that kind of exposure could elevate their business." Marietta shrugged. "Well, at least one of them did."

I almost choked on the chunk of muffin in my mouth. "What's that supposed to mean?"

My mother answered with another shrug. "Veronica seemed very clear-eyed about the potential of the show. In one of her emails she even called it free advertising."

I dropped the rest of my muffin to my plate. Again. "You two exchanged emails about this?"

She nodded. "Almost every day leading up to Thanksgiving."

That didn't sound like someone who would want to get rid of her business partner. "Do you still have them?"

"Of course." Marietta picked up her phone and scrolled her email app. "Veronica brought up a couple of things I wanted to pass along to my agent. One of them was quite savvy. Really showed that she was doing her homework." She tapped her phone with a blood-red lacquered nail. "Was it this one? Hmm... Maybe it was one from the day before."

I didn't care how well-versed the woman seemed about the reality television industry. I was only interested in what Veronica Lovely might have to say about her husband.

I snatched the phone from her hand. "May I?"

"Charmaine!" she protested. "Do I read your personal correspondence?"

"You already told us that this was business-related, and now that this idea of yours is a no-go, there's no harm in me seeing what she had to say, is there?"

Slumping in her chair, Marietta folded her arms tight under her double Ds. "I suppose not."

Good, because I intended to read every word.

The first thing that struck me while reading Veronica Lovely's email from Tuesday was how precise she was with her language. It was as if I was reading a business letter composed by one of the prosecuting attorneys I worked with. It was direct and to the point. No emojis. No text talk acronyms. There was also no mention of her husband, which I found rather curious since Kevin was very much alive at the time she and my mother were exchanging emails.

Instead, Veronica posed the sort of questions I would want answered prior to getting involved in a business deal with my mother.

Okay, no matter how she answered those questions, I didn't know that I'd ever get involved in a business deal with Marietta. Our relationship was already complicated enough.

Still, they were good questions, seemingly asked to gauge how serious Marietta was about promoting the show concept to her agent.

Then, after my mother wrote back telling her that they had already spoken about it and that the next step would be a video conference with her agent, Veronica responded early Wednesday morning.

Excellent. I can make myself available anytime next week, after the holiday.

"I just need to get rid of my husband first," I muttered under my breath as I forwarded the email chain to myself. Not that it contained anything Ben Santiago would find especially suspicious, but if there was even a remote possibility that Veronica Lovely could be criminally charged for the death of her husband, I wanted to preserve it as evidence.

"What are you doing?" Marietta snatched her phone from my hands. "You said you were just going to look."

"I just needed…" And was failing to come up with an excuse for copying her email that my mother would buy. "I thought we might want to follow up with Veronica about updating the rental," I said, referring to the bungalow I had been renting from Barry for the last thirteen months. "And I wanted to make sure I had her email address."

Fixing her gaze on me like a disapproving parent, Gram shook her head.

Yes, I know. That was lame, but I didn't want to say

anything to give my mother the impression that I was in any way involved in Kevin Lovely's death investigation.

Marietta frowned as much as her latest Botox injection would allow. "Barry hasn't wanted to discuss making any updates to either house. I really don't understand it. He and I are usually on the same page about these matters."

I didn't find it difficult to understand. My mother hadn't worked for months, having turned down any part that conflicted with my September wedding date. Which she liked to remind me of as a show of proof that she had made me and my wedding her top priority.

And until I provided her with a new wedding date, she seemed determined to continue to demonstrate her commitment, no matter how crazy it made the rest of us. Including her latest husband, my former high school biology teacher, who couldn't be keen on the idea of spending more than he earned in a year on a bunch of unnecessary renovations.

"So I wouldn't suggest following up with Veronica about the house or anything else referenced in those emails," Marietta added, staring down at her phone as if she were trying to convince herself of the wisdom of her advice.

Swallowing the last bite of my muffin, I scooted closer to get a better read of her face. "You mean her interest in your show idea."

My mother dropped the phone to the table. "She was definitely interested. You read what she wrote. She wanted to move forward with the meeting with my agent."

"But I thought Kevin didn't want to do that," Gram said. "And if he—"

"Even if he didn't, he's not around to object to the idea now." I cringed at how callous I sounded, but I suspected Marietta only heard me echo what she had been thinking.

The tugs at the corners of her Cupid's bow mouth told me that I had just hit the bull's-eye. "Charmaine, really. Is that any way to speak of the dearly departed?"

I leaned back in my chair. "I know. I'm just saying that if you think she could pull off hosting the show by herself, maybe this doesn't have to be a done deal."

"Oh, Veronica could do it," Marietta stated emphatically. "I have no doubt that she could do anything she set her mind to."

Such as eliminate a lying cheat of a husband? "Maybe you could pay her a visit to extend your condolences and that subject could come up."

My mother's lips stretched into a sly smile. "Maybe I could."

"I could even bake a cake and go with you so that it seems more like the family offering their condolences."

"That would be nice," Gram chimed in.

Marietta shrugged dismissively. "Oh, I don't know if that's necessary. I'm sure I can handle it by myself."

"Really? You want to drive there and back in the rain?" Because after totaling two cars, my mother tended to white-knuckle the rare occasions she got behind the wheel. "Plus, you'd be driving to a remote location you've never been to before. Possibly in the dark."

She huffed in resignation. "Fine."

I seconded that fine and made a mental note to stop at the grocery store on the way home.

I needed to bake a cake for Heather's chief suspect.

Chapter Seven

"Now remember, let me do the talking," Marietta said as she used my passenger side mirror to fluff her spiky auburn hair. "I told Veronica when we would be stopping by, but I didn't explain in my email who I was bringing with me. Which shouldn't be a big deal. I'll introduce you as my daughter and then I expect you to be on your best behavior."

From the moment I picked her up after work Monday, my mother had been recycling the instructions I used to hear on the rare occasions she'd drag me to one of her public events.

At least this time I knew I wouldn't have to dutifully smile at any cameras. Which was just as well. After getting caught in a sudden downpour while delivering a subpoena a few hours earlier, my hair and makeup weren't camera-ready, unlike my mother's.

"You don't need to talk to me like I'm ten. I get the fact that I'm mainly along for the ride." Even though I was the one doing the driving, which made me wish that I had chosen my words more carefully, especially since

Marietta was giving me some serious side-eye.

"This visit is important to me, Charmaine." She flipped up the visor with more force than necessary. "Depending on how our discussion goes, it could lead to a new chapter in my career. Maybe even my own production company, so I'm simply asking that you not try to dominate the conversation with any probing questions about Kevin's unfortunate demise."

"Excuse me?" I had no intention of being so obvious. "I've never met the woman before, so I'd hardly know what to say to her beyond offering my condolences."

Marietta gave me a long look as I took the left turn to climb the winding, tree-lined lane that led to Veronica Lovely's house. "Somehow, I doubt that."

"What's that supposed to mean?"

"You invited yourself along for a reason."

I slowed when I rounded a bend and the beam of my headlights illuminated skid marks that led to a clearing between two massive cedar trees. "Let's not—"

"Whatever are you looking at?" She sucked in a sharp breath. "Is that it? Where he went off the road?"

It had to have been. "It's dark, so it's hard to say."

"Well, *some* vehicle certainly went off the road there, and if this is the street where Kevin lived, it stands to reason it was his car, doesn't it?"

My mother was applying too much logic for my comfort level.

"It could have been, but I really don't know for sure." Ben had been in court most of the day, and Steve hadn't wanted to hear another word about Heather's suspicions, so I didn't know any more than I did yesterday.

"I thought you were a death investigator," Marietta said as we wound our way up a hill. "Shouldn't you know these things?"

"I help with investigations when the coroner needs more information to determine the cause of death. This was an accident." The investigation conclusion that Steve wanted me to remind Heather of the next time I saw her.

Hoping that would end the discussion about my job, I headed for the streetlamp at the end of the cul-de-sac.

"A tragic accident," my mother said as we pulled into the driveway of a house with charcoal gray shutters and dormer windows upstairs, and red brick wrapped around the downstairs picture window. "But truly just a car accident, right? Nothing more to it than that?"

That depended upon who I talked to. "Nope."

Marietta smirked at me. "Then why did you really want to come here today?"

Logical Marietta was really starting to get on my nerves.

Smiling sweetly, I parked the car what I figured would be a safe distance away from the portable basketball hoop at the top of the drive. "I'm just here to support you."

"Sure you are."

"And carry the cake," I said, reaching into the back for the pink pastry box I had picked up at Duke's yesterday so I wouldn't need to leave my cake carrier.

"I thought you baked that cake."

"I did."

"That box makes it look like we bought it."

Good grief. "It doesn't matter. It's just cake."

"That you made for the occasion," she said, leading the way to the front door while a dog loudly protested our arrival from the fenced backyard. "That shows a level of caring—that some thought and effort went into it."

Hardly any thought had gone into the chocolate layer cake. I had baked others like it more times than I could count. I simply made the favorite cake from my childhood with the hope that it would be something Veronica's kids would enjoy.

Marietta gave me a wink as she pressed the doorbell, igniting a flurry of deep woofs in the back. "I'll mention that you baked the cake."

"No need." Because that was the last thing I wanted to talk about in there.

She cast a worried glance toward the dark side yard. "He does not sound happy to have visitors."

I was sure he wouldn't be the only member of the Lovely household to feel that way.

A few seconds later, a boy with shaggy brown hair appeared at the door. He looked to be around twelve years old, and I assumed he must have been the one to witness his father's accident.

Marietta leaned over to make herself eye level with him. "Hello there. Is your mother home?"

I stifled a groan when I heard her drop the *r* in *mother*. The fake southern accent she used at all her personal appearances was back in full force.

The kid's eyebrows collided as if he wanted as little to do with her southern-fried persona as I did.

"Mom!" he called out a split second later. Then he ran up a gleaming oak staircase and disappeared into a back room, leaving the front door open to reveal an expensive-looking Persian area rug in the same rich red tones as the brick outside, and entryway walls painted in a bold pomegranate.

Directly across from us, under a pendulum wall clock sat a framed family photo on an antique console table. A handsome, dark-haired man in his mid-thirties held a grinning toddler while a much younger version of the boy leaned his head against his smiling mom's shoulder.

They looked like the perfect, happy family. Then.

But I knew better than most that appearances could be deceiving.

"Nice, don't you think?" my mother whispered. "I knew from the moment I met Veronica that she had exquisite taste."

"Yep." The Lovely home made quite the first impression. I wasn't so sure that I could say the same thing for the woman in the baggy, stained jeans and plaid flannel shirt shuffling toward us in fleece-lined slippers.

Her pale lips curled as if she were on hostess autopilot while her amber eyes held a steady but unwelcoming gaze, especially when it landed on me.

Tucking back a chunk of shoulder-length coffee-brown hair behind her ear, she shifted her attention to my mother. "Ms. Moreau, it's so good of you to come."

"Call me Marietta, please," she said, stepping onto the

rug. "We're all friends here."

Based on how Veronica was staring at me, my mother was being too generous with her friendship circle.

An introduction was definitely in order.

I waited, looking at Marietta, but she only had eyes for the pair of scalloped glass sconces bookending the clock.

Seriously, Mom?

I had to say something to break the awkward silence and noticed a short row of kids' shoes to the right of the door. "Should we take off our shoes?"

Veronica waved me off with a hand that sported a sparkling diamond solitaire. "I only insist that my children remove their shoes since they can't seem to remember to wipe their feet."

To make sure I didn't track in any of the fall foliage the earlier rainstorm had dropped onto the front porch, I gave the soles of my ankle boots another wipe on her welcome mat and offered her a smile that wasn't returned. Instead, she closed the door behind me and silently led the way to a huge kitchen that looked like it should be showcased in *Better Homes and Gardens.*

"May I offer you some tea or coffee?" Veronica asked as she stepped to a claw-footed table in the breakfast nook and pulled out one of the four padded chairs for my mother.

"No, we don't want you to go to any trouble." Marietta motioned for me to join her at the table while a Great Dane barked at her from the other side of a slider door.

"Rocky, no bark!" Veronica commanded, closing the

blinds over the door.

While our hostess had her back to me, I gave my mother a hard stare. *Aren't you forgetting something?*

Marietta cocked her pretty head and mouthed, *What?*

I clenched my teeth because the woman who had wanted to do all the talking picked a fine time to give me the silent treatment.

"Sorry about that," Veronica said. "He's a good guard dog, but we're still working on his training."

Something that obviously wasn't a priority right now. What was a priority was an introduction or this visit was going to become increasingly awkward.

"I could say the same about my dog. And I'm sorry, I don't think we've met. I'm Charmaine, Marietta's daughter, and on behalf of the family we wanted to offer our condolences." I set the pastry box in the center of a gleaming slab of cream and cocoa granite.

"You're very kind. We appreciate it." Veronica's voice was emotionless, her body very still as if she were conserving her energy in order to make polite conversation.

Based on the makeup smudges under her heavy-lidded eyes, I wondered when she last slept.

"My daughter made the cake," Marietta blurted out as if she had suddenly remembered one of her lines. "She used to be a pastry chef, so you know it's going to be good."

Again, not what I wanted to talk about.

"And what do you do now?" Veronica asked.

Not an unreasonable question to ask, but absolutely, positively, not what I wanted to talk about.

"I work for the county. Mainly admin-type stuff." I didn't want any follow-up questions, so I tried to make it sound as boring as possible. "Nothing that allows me to be creative like the two of you." I pointed at the multi-color paint splatters on her jeans. "In fact, it looks like we might have interrupted you."

Veronica looked down as if she had forgotten what she was wearing. "Oh, I was just painting one of the rooms upstairs. With the shop closed so that I could be here for my kids, I needed something to occupy my mind."

I wondered if that room had been the bedroom she had shared with her husband. If my cheat of an ex-husband had died prior to our divorce, I would have wanted to strip my bedroom bare and redecorate it with a palette of feminine pastels that he would have hated. Maybe not three days after I saw him drive away for the last time, but we do what we need to navigate through the crises in our lives.

"Of course you did. Why, I imagine you've been run-nin' yourself ragged the last few days." Marietta gestured to the chair next to her. "Please, sit. Unless, of course, you'd like some cake, in which case Charmaine would be happy to—"

"No." Veronica gave me an apologetic glance. "I'm sure it's delicious, but since the accident I haven't had the stomach for much more than tea and crackers."

Given how low her baggy jeans hung from her slender hips, I believed her. In fact, I hadn't picked up on any-thing the least bit *off* about the woman.

Sure, she had been guarded when she had first en-countered a stranger at her door. I would have been, too. I didn't make any more out of that than I did the fact that, unlike Heather, Kevin's widow didn't look as if she had spent most of the weekend in tears over his passing. The only time I saw Gram cry after we lost my grandfather was at his funeral.

Veronica struck me as the kind of professional who possessed the skill to shift her emotions into neutral when dealing with difficult clients. I didn't doubt that she could do the same when dealing with a difficult situation for her family. That would make her body language a bit more challenging to read.

But not impossible, I thought as I followed her to the table and took the seat across from her.

"It will take some time," Marietta said, reaching out to pat Veronica's hand. "Matters of the heart always do. In the meantime, I think you're smart to stay busy."

Casting her gaze to the tabletop, Veronica withdrew her hand. "I don't know about smart, but it seems to help me get through the day."

My mother lowered her voice. "Forgive me if it's too soon, but I wanted to talk to you about something else that could help. And I don't want to be indelicate. You just lost your husband—your partner—and while I thought the two of you together would make a wonderful team doing what you do..." Marietta winced at her faux pas. "What you *did* in front of the camera. There's no reason why that can't still happen."

"I-I don't understand." Veronica's eyes narrowed as I

might have expected from someone trying to focus on the message my mother was conveying instead of her fake accent.

At the same time, Veronica gave her head a little shake—something a lot of us do when we need more information to fully comprehend what we've been told.

If I hadn't been watching her so carefully, I never would have doubted her sincerity. Because the businesswoman who had sent that email to declare her interest in hosting that show was good at reading the room.

She knew that the only audience member she needed to care about right now was Marietta, who was trying to keep hope alive in a grieving widow.

What my mother didn't know was that she didn't need to try so hard.

Hope was very much alive as evidenced by the flicker of the smile tugging at Veronica's lips.

Did the fact that she could compartmentalize her emotions make her a bad person?

Nope. Far from it.

But the smile that Veronica failed to suppress sent up a red flag—one that I wouldn't have given a second thought to if Heather hadn't sent me here to root out her lover's killer.

"I would like to go forward with the meeting we discussed. Not this week, of course, but..." Marietta said, pausing when the front door shut with a thud.

Veronica shifted in her seat to cast a worried glance out the dining room front window at her son bouncing a basketball under an outside light. "It's okay. That was just Jonah. He hasn't been easy with doors this week. Anyway, you were saying?"

Yes, this was a discussion she definitely wanted to continue.

I knew it was the same with my mother. And since she had made it abundantly clear that I was to be a good little girl and let the grownups talk, this seemed like the perfect opportunity for me to get to know one of the other kids around here.

Specifically, the one who had witnessed the accident.

Grabbing my keys from my tote bag, I pushed away from the table. "Excuse me for a few minutes. I'm just going to move my car to give him more room out there."

Marietta waved me away as if I were interrupting her train of thought.

Ordinarily, I would have found her dismissal annoying, but since she was giving me leave, I didn't hesitate to head out to where Jonah was standing behind a yellow chalk line illuminated by a flood light. I waited until he sank his basket to make a move.

"Nice shot," I said, rattling my keys so that he wouldn't think I had come out here just to talk to him.

Jonah retrieved his ball, holding it in front of his chest like a shield. "Thanks."

I noticed he was wearing a familiar-looking black and gold Hagen Middle School sweatshirt and envied him its warmth since I had left my jacket in the house.

"I have that same sweatshirt from when I went there." At least I'd had something similar two decades ago that I had long since grown out of.

He seemed to be avoiding eye contact with me, much like my ex-husband at our divorce settlement. He tried to play it cool as if he needed to shutter his eyes to my presence.

Probably because Chris knew I could see right through him.

It was the same with this skinny kid, with one major difference. Other than having attended the same middle school, we had no common history, nothing that should have given him a reason to be particularly wary of me.

Of course, Jonah had just experienced the most traumatic event of his young life, so maybe he wasn't as shuttered as he was emotionally numb.

I pasted a friendly smile on my face. "What grade are you in?"

"Seventh," Jonah muttered.

Doing some quick mental math, I figured that I had guessed right. He was around twelve years old. "Do you play for the Warriors?"

He nodded.

Really. They certainly didn't put him on the team for his height because I towered over him in my two-inch boot heels.

"Cool. I used to play." Softball, but he didn't need to know that.

I pocketed my keys and pointed at the chalk line. "Want to practice your outside shot? I'll get the rebounds."

Jonah's big eyes darkened with suspicion. "You don't

have to."

"I know, but our moms are talking right now, and I thought they could use some privacy for a few minutes. So if you don't mind me hanging out here with you for a little while..."

He shrugged, but started dribbling, so I took that for a yes.

A second later, he jumped and sank the ball through the hoop.

"Pretty good." I bounced the ball back to him.

After he made three baskets in a row, I clapped and immediately understood how this little kid could have made the team. "Okay, showoff, let's see if you can make it from the top of the key."

Jonah held his head a bit higher as he jogged back a few steps to take his shot.

Which was good. He was enjoying having an audience, maybe even feeling like a normal kid for the first time since his father's accident.

The ball bounced off the rim and rolled toward my car, which gave me a welcome chance to generate some body heat by running after it. "Close." I passed him the ball. "Try that again."

This time he made the shot.

"Two points, but the defender fouled you, so step to the line to make it three." I handed Jonah the ball as if I were the referee. "Okay, the game's tied and there's only one second left, so this is your moment of glory."

Jonah bounced the ball three times and then heaved it toward the dimly lit backboard, where it circled the hoop to add to the drama of our little game before it dropped in.

"Yay!" I ran to the grinning seventh-grader and high-fived him. "You're the game hero!"

The grin fell from his lips as if I had slapped his face instead of his hand.

"It's dark. We should probably go in," Jonah said, retrieving the ball.

I wasn't sure what had happened to cause him to shut down so abruptly. But his somber expression told me it had nothing to do with basketball.

I doubted that he would want to talk to me about it, but I thought I should try.

Unlocking my car doors with my remote so that the headlights would come on, I called after Jonah, "I need to get something from my car first. In fact, it's so dark, would you mind walking me out there?"

He rolled the ball into a pile of leaves collecting in the landscaping and followed me to my Subaru.

"When's your next game?" I asked as I popped the hatch with the hope that I had left something in the cargo hold that I could use as a prop.

"Friday."

I turned to face him. "I'm really sorry that your dad won't be there to see you play."

Jonah pressed his lips together, working his mouth as if the words it contained dare not leak out.

Taking a step back, he stared down at his Nikes, but not before I could see the flash of anger on his face.

I didn't want to press this kid too hard. He had suffered enough. He didn't need me picking at the edges of what had to feel like an open wound. "More than that, I'm just sorry for everything that you're going through right now."

"You don't know what I'm going through." Jonah bolted, shouting as he ran toward the house. "You don't know anything at all!"

He wasn't wrong. I couldn't imagine how his world had shifted on its axis.

Closing the hatch of my Subaru, I went inside to see if my mother was ready to leave. Because I sure was.

Chapter Eight

Since I was arriving home two hours later than most weeknights, I had expected to hear my hungry dog anxiously barking to be let in. But when I spotted Steve's Ford F150 truck gleaming like gunmetal under the streetlight on my corner, I knew I'd find Fozzie happy in his company, and I smiled for the first time since leaving Veronica Lovely's house.

Steve often swung by on his way home from work, so this wasn't a rare occurrence, just a very welcome one. And the anticipation of holding him tight immediately lifted my spirits after a long, miserable day—a day I had made ten times worse by manipulating my mother to get inside a grieving widow's home.

Of course, Marietta had thought that our visit with Veronica Lovely couldn't have gone better. She had managed to resuscitate her reality show idea back to life, so her mission had been accomplished.

My mother had been positively giddy on the drive back to her house. And why wouldn't she be? She wouldn't be the one replaying Jonah's accusations when her head hit her pillow tonight.

He had been right. I didn't know anything, and I didn't want to pry into the circumstances surrounding his father's death more than I already had. Which was exactly what I was going to tell Heather after I mustered enough energy to respond to one of the three texts she had sent me over the course of the last twenty-four hours.

She wanted an update and would probably show up at my door tomorrow if I didn't hurry up and provide her one. But first, I had a cop waiting for me inside, who could provide me with some sweet distraction from all the drama Heather had sucked me into.

At least, that was what I had been hoping for when I stepped through the back door. But of the two males in my kitchen, only the one wagging his fluffy tail looked happy to see me. The other one appeared to be conducting a search of my refrigerator.

"You have nothing to eat in here," Steve announced as if he were waiting for a grocery delivery to magically fill the space between the half-empty egg carton and a bottle of salad dressing.

"Sure I do." With Fozzie trailing at my feet, I reached around Steve to open the vegetable bin. "I have lettuce, carrots, tomatoes, and a cucumber."

He immediately closed the bin. "Rabbit food."

"Toss on some of that dressing and it's a delicious salad."

"Yeah, right."

To provide myself the distraction I had been craving,

I reached up, linked my hands behind his neck, and gave him a kiss. "Maybe you should have let me know you were coming. I could have picked something up for us on my way home."

"I did," he said while Fozzie tried to wedge between us. "I texted you when I left the station twenty minutes ago."

"Oh." I had assumed that was another text from Heather.

I leaned over to hug Fozzie around the ruff and give him the attention he was demanding. "I was on the road at the time. Just shows I wasn't texting and driving. Doesn't it, boy?"

He woofed and then lay down at Steve's feet as if he were picking a side between Mom and Dad.

Turncoat. "And I'd like to state for the record, officer, that I happened to be obeying the other rules of the road, too."

Glancing up at Steve, I noticed he didn't look amused. I had a very bad feeling I was about to find out why.

Leaning back against my tile counter, he folded his arms against his chest. "Where've you been?"

"I was sort of running an errand with my mother." A fool's errand that I really regretted and hoped he wouldn't ask any questions about, because I didn't want to lie to the man I loved.

"Sort of?"

"You know, because she's a horrible driver and none of us want her behind the wheel, especially at night."

"This wouldn't have anything to do with Heather,

would it?"

Crap. "Why would time that I'm spending with my mother have anything to do with Heather?"

"I don't know." Steve reached into the back pocket of his chinos for his cell phone and tapped on it. "But I got this text from her a half hour ago, and I quote, 'Do you know where Char is?' Interesting timing, don't you think?"

Crapity, crap, crap, crap.

"How sweet." I forced a smile. "It's almost as if she likes me again."

"What's going on between you two?"

"It's not a girl crush. You have nothing to worry about."

He cocked his head at me, his brow furrowed, while Fozzie whimpered, no doubt sensing the rising tension in the kitchen.

"I know, you're hungry," I said to Fozzie and then ducked into the pantry to put some distance between Steve and me.

"I already fed him, so stop stalling. What are you two up to?"

"Nothing, really. Like I said, I was helping my mother with something." I cringed because that sounded like an evasive answer. Probably because it was one.

"Okay, he's been fed, so let's talk about our dinner." *Please.*

I retrieved a can of soup from the pantry shelf and turned to face my inquisitor. "Soup and salad is pretty much all I can offer you unless you want to have breakfast for dinner. I could scramble—"

"Soup and salad's fine." Steve grabbed the can from my hands, set it on the counter and then led me to the kitchen table, where he pulled out a chair. "Enough with the diversion tactics. What don't you want to tell me?"

When I took a seat, Fozzie did the same, only at the doorway to the hall so that he could make himself scarce if he wanted to.

I didn't have that option, so the only thing left for me was to clear the air. More or less.

"There's not a lot to say. But first of all, I'm sorry Heather bothered you with that text." Really sorry. "She's having a hard time accepting that Kevin Lovely's death was an accident. Such a hard time that when she couldn't reach you on Saturday, she talked to me about it."

His dark eyes narrowed. "She never talks to you."

I shrugged. "I guess she called a truce."

"Why? What did you do?"

"Me?! You were the one who made himself unavailable to her. All day, I might add. So, out of desperation, I guess she staked out your house, and then spotted me when I arrived to take my grandmother shopping. That's when I got to hear all about how you weren't returning her calls."

"Don't even try to pin this on me."

"I'm not." Okay, maybe I was deflecting a little bit. "I'm just saying that she was upset and seemed to need someone to talk to."

"Uh-huh."

"I was just trying to be a decent human being."

"Right."

"You don't believe me? You can ask Gram about this. She was there."

"I don't need any corroborating witnesses. I believe you."

"You don't sound like you do."

"I just have the sense that there's a lot more to this story."

As was typical, his spidey senses were right on the money.

"For example." Steve locked his gaze on mine. "This 'sort of' errand you were running with your mother. Could you be any more vague?"

Oh, I was sure I could if I tried.

"I just didn't want to bore you with the details. You know how you get when I mention the stuff she's working on."

He smirked. "Yeah."

I pointed at his chiseled lips. "That's the reaction I get every time."

The smirk didn't budge. "I promise I won't be bored."

"It's not a done deal yet, so I don't know that she'd want me to say anything—"

"You're stalling again, which can only mean one thing. You don't want me to know where you went."

Exactly right.

"And since this seems to have something to do with Heather, who refuses to accept the fact that the guy she was seeing died from the injuries he sustained in a car accident... Let me think." Steve stroked the dark stubble on his chin. "What do Heather and your mother have in common?"

"Besides a history of getting involved with unavailable men?"

"Yeah, besides that."

"Fine." I couldn't tap dance around the truth any longer. "We went to see Veronica Lovely. Partly to offer our condolences, but my mother mainly wanted to talk to her about that reality show—how that idea didn't have to die just because Kevin did."

"Whoa. I never thought of your mother as being cold-blooded before, but—"

"She's not. She thought she was giving Veronica something positive to think about—something that she had clearly been interested in. You should have seen the emails that went back and forth between them. They were just about to set up a meeting with my mom's agent and then Kevin had his accident."

"Whatever."

"So she was using this opportunity to try to keep hope alive for both their sakes."

Steve took in a breath and slowly released it. "And what were you trying to do?"

"I don't know." I hung my head to avoid the accusation in his eyes. "I guess I just wanted to meet Veronica after hearing so much about her."

"From Heather."

And Lucille, who I knew better than to mention, so I just nodded.

"I suppose she wanted you to find out the truth about what *really* happened," Steve said as if it were a forgone conclusion.

"Something like that."

"So what are you going to tell her when she calls? Because I happen to know from personal experience, that's what happens if you don't respond to her texts."

I groaned with the certainty that would be my fate if I didn't provide a response to Heather's last text post-haste. "I really don't want to talk to her." And definitely not tonight.

I pulled out my phone from the tote bag slung over the back of my chair. "I'll send Heather a quick text to let her know that I didn't find out anything to support her suspicions. She won't be happy about it, but it's the truth, whether she chooses to accept it or not."

"Oh, I guarantee she won't be happy about it. So don't be surprised if she goes back to giving you the silent treatment."

"So what else is new?" I said as I typed.

Seconds after I hit *send* my phone started ringing. "Criminy!" I exclaimed when I recognized Heather's phone number. "What more is there to say?!"

Pushing out of his chair, Steve kissed the top of my head. "I'll get the salad started."

Chapter Nine

After Steve headed home around ten, I changed into my favorite cuddly pajamas and settled onto my sofa to watch *Pretty Woman*.

I thought spending a couple of hours with Julia Roberts and Richard Gere would improve my mood. Then, maybe I could shut down my brain and get some sleep.

I thought the same thing about the pint of chocolate chip cookie dough ice cream I fetched from my freezer midway through the movie.

It turned out I was wrong on both counts.

There was nothing that could improve my mood after hearing my former best friend tearfully accuse me of taking Veronica Lovely's side against her.

"I should have known better than to trust you!" were the last words Heather said to me.

And I didn't know why they hurt as much as they did.

As Steve had been quick to point out when we went out for a walk with Fozzie after dinner, Heather had come to me in desperation, wanting to find someone to blame for the death of her lover. She had been asking for the impossible, so it wasn't my fault that I had nothing to give her.

It just felt like my fault.

Which only compounded the guilt I felt for inserting myself in the middle of the Lovely family's grief.

I wished I could have a do-over of Saturday so that Heather would have gone back to her car to wait for Steve, and I wouldn't have let my curiosity get the best of me.

But no! I had to jump into this miserable mess with both my size eights.

"I don't know what I can do about it now," I said to the dog following me to my bedroom after the movie ended.

I said the same thing after tossing and turning for the next couple of hours.

Fozzie had no answers for me when I stepped over him on my way to the closet for my robe. Instead, I got a huff of displeasure for interrupting his slumber.

"If you're trying to make me feel guilty, you're gonna have to take a number. My guilt tank is already full. But do you know what might make me feel better? We should go for a run."

He yawned.

Okay, in all honesty I didn't want to go either. Especially after I peeked through my bedroom blinds and saw the steady drizzle illuminated by the streetlight.

Instead, I let Fozzie out into the backyard, brewed a pot of French roast, took a long, hot shower, and got ready to face the day. Even after I spent some extra time to flat-iron the curls out of my hair and apply enough makeup to appear somewhat lifelike, I still had over an hour to kill before the Chimacam County sheriff's deputy working security would unlock the courthouse doors.

I thought about using the time to catch up on my laundry, and then my stomach rumbled, informing me that a better use of my time might be scrambling a couple of eggs for breakfast.

Protein packed and sensible considering the diet I was supposed to be on, but also boring.

I opened my mostly empty refrigerator to see if I had anything to go with those eggs.

Like bacon.

Not necessarily part of a sensible breakfast, which was a moot point since I didn't have any.

But I knew where I could find some.

"Good morning," I sang out ten minutes later, when the Duke's Cafe kitchen screen door banged shut behind me.

My great-aunt Alice looked up from the flour she was scooping into a commercial stand mixing bowl. "Well, well. Somebody's up early."

She watched as I stowed my tote in my old locker and hung up my dripping coat, exchanging it for one of the white aprons hanging on a hook near the door.

"Uh-oh." Alice scowled. "If you're putting that on, it can only mean one thing."

"That I plan to eat breakfast here," I said as I fastened the apron tie around the waistband of my charcoal gray wool trousers. "But I thought I should help with the baking or else your husband will think I'm a freeloader."

Duke chortled from the worktable where he was dipping this morning's batch of apple fritters into a pan of glaze. "Like that will change my opinion of you after all these years."

"Never mind him." Alice slanted a glance at the clock mounted above the vintage red and white Coca-Cola sign. "It's not even six o'clock and you're all put together, like you've got a hot date."

Her inference being that I didn't usually look this good so early in the morning, which I knew was true. I was also pretty sure that she didn't mean it as a compliment.

Blocking my path to the mixing bowls stacked behind her table, Alice squinted at me through her wire-rimmed trifocals. "Are you wearing your mother's purple eye shadow?"

It was Midnight Sun Mauve from the cosmetic line Marietta hawked on late-night infomercials. According to her, the shadow base along with the coordinating liner was supposed to make my bleary eyes pop with subtle shimmer.

Two hours ago, I thought I could use all the pop I could get. Now, with the way Alice was scrutinizing my face, I wondered if I'd gone overboard in the shimmer department. "Maybe a little."

Duke walked over, wiping his hands on a kitchen rag

as he gave me a head-to-toe once-over. "What're you all dolled up for?"

"And so early, too," Alice added. "Is something going on that we don't know about?"

I had no desire to admit to why I was trying to feel better about myself this morning. "Nope."

Disappointment pulled at my great-aunt's mouth. "There's nothing special happening later?"

"It's just a normal Tuesday." That's what I was hoping for, anyway.

Alice inched closer. "Then do you have some big plans for later in the week?"

"Big plans?" I should have consumed enough caffeine for my synapses to be firing on all cylinders, but I didn't understand what she was asking. "Am I supposed to have some 'big plans'?"

"Told ya," Duke crowed, heading toward the bakery case with his tray of apple fritters.

"I know, I know," Alice called after him. "I shouldn't believe every rumor I hear."

What?! "There's a rumor going around about me?"

She waved me off. "It's nothing. Probably just idle speculation."

"About?"

"Oh, sweetie, it's not worth repeating." After a quick pat on my shoulder, Alice returned to her mixer.

My breath caught in my throat. "It's that bad?"

"No, truly it's nothing." She shot me the look that she used to remind me that she was the boss of her kitchen. "So just let it be."

But I wasn't fifteen and she was no longer the boss of me. "Just tell me."

"Fine!" Grimacing, Alice carried the mixing bowl back to her butcher block worktable and then took her usual seat.

I slipped onto the wooden stool across from her. "So what is this nothing-burger?"

"Okay, the way it was relayed to me—"

"By whom?"

She leveled her gaze at me. "Lucille, who else? And she'll be here in a few minutes, so don't let on that I told you."

"She swore you to secrecy?"

Alice nodded.

Good grief. "Okay, let's have it."

"Well, what Luce told me was that someone had it on good authority that you and Steve were..." She lowered her voice to a whisper. "Eloping."

"Eloping!" What the heck! Did Gossip Central have such a slow news day that someone decided to make up a story about me and Steve?

At least it was a small mercy that this rumor had nothing to do with the death of Kevin Lovely.

"And when you came in all gussied up, I thought to-day might be the day," Alice said.

"Well, it's not. It's just a normal workday." Although it was feeling less normal by the second.

Alice leaned in. "So you two aren't eloping?"

"Not that I know of."

"I should've known that she had it all wrong."

"Who? Lucille?"

"Evie Bukowski? Bartowski? Whatever the heck the name of that new math teacher is that Barry works with. You know, the one he mentioned that he'd taken under his wing when we were there for Thanksgiving."

I had the sinking feeling some dots were about to be connected to the announcement that didn't happen that night.

"Anyway, I guess she came in for a takeout order when Steve was here yesterday, and she asked Luce who he was. She made it sound like Evie what's-her-name was looking at him with a little too much interest, so she told her he was engaged."

I didn't think Steve needed Lucille's help fending off his female admirers, but I knew her heart was in the right place. "And then Evie said…"

"Something about being surprised to see him here because the two of you were supposed to be eloping."

The only reason she would have thought such a thing was because my newest stepfather repeated something he had jokingly suggested last Thursday. That if we eloped, Marietta would finally stop needling me to set a date for the wedding.

"She had to have heard something wrong." And I wasn't the only one in my family who needed to learn to keep their mouth shut.

"That's exactly what your granny said when I called her about it. I told Lucille not to repeat what she'd heard to anybody. That it was a bunch of hooey. But I'm afraid I was too late."

Uh-oh. "What did Lucille do?"

Alice cringed. "You know how she is when it's a juicy rumor about someone she's interested in. I swear the woman is like a dog with a bone. She doesn't rest until she gets corroboration."

Grinding my molars, I braced for what was coming. "Please don't tell me that she called any of my friends."

"Okay." Alice peered into her mixing bowl like she wanted to hide in the cake batter. "I won't tell you that."

I glared in the direction of the back door as it banged shut.

"Goody!" Lucille pointed at me. "Just the person I wanted to see this morning."

"Same here." I patted the stool next to me. "Have a seat."

Chapter Ten

Almost six hours later, I bellied up to the bar at Eddie's Place, the former brick warehouse that my friends Eddie and Roxanne Fiske had transformed into an eight-lane bowling alley and tavern.

Eddie's was the place to go to for the best pizza in town, and truth be told, it rivaled Duke's when it came to juicy bacon cheeseburgers. But I'd had my fill of bacon and cheese earlier, when my great-uncle surprised me with an omelet on the house to thank me for helping restock their bakery case.

He clearly hadn't been aware of the apple fritter I snitched for a mid-morning snack. And since the only exercise I'd gotten in today, aside from walking to the third-floor breakroom to make coffee, was dashing to my car between raindrops, the last thing I needed was a big, greasy lunch.

But I wasn't here to eat.

I needed to talk to my best friend—the pretty one standing on the other side of the unoccupied oak bar with her hands on her hips.

"Don't you look nice," Roxanne said with a twinkle in her cocoa brown eyes. "You wouldn't have some big plans after work that you came over to tell me about, would you?"

"If there were any truth to that rumor about us eloping, you know you would have been the first to hear about it." I reached for one of the laminated menus stacked at the end of the bar. "You also know that my grandmother would never forgive me if I deprived her of seeing me marry Steve."

Rox tossed a paper coaster in front of me, placed a glass coffee mug on it without me having to ask, and started pouring. "Trust me, there are quite a few of us looking forward to that day. So, when's it gonna be?"

I hung my head. "I don't know."

"Char, it's been over two months."

"That much I do know."

"As much as I think your ex is a total jerk, he didn't intentionally ruin your wedding. It was just a freaky coincidence."

"I know that, too." Just like I knew that the stars didn't align to stop me from marrying Steve. It had only seemed a little like the woo-woo stuff my mother bought into—something that could have been interpreted as a warning from the universe.

So, I heeded the warning.

My wedding was now a "TBD" event that I had parked a safe distance away in the future, which was supposed to give me time to come up with a new plan. And to get my head screwed on straight. To think about what I really wanted. All things I'd thought I had needed eight weeks ago.

Now I wasn't so sure. About anything.

I glanced over at Ernie Kozarek and two of his bowling buddies wearing powder blue-striped team shirts taking one of the tables near the entrance. Two more seniors I recognized as pals of Duke's followed, accompanied by the sound of the rumbles and crashes coming from the remaining occupied lanes.

"Looks like the senior league has worked up an appetite." Rox grabbed several menus since Sofia, her waitress, had her hands full delivering a large takeout order to one of the guys from the county clerk's office standing near the register. "Let me get their drink orders and I'll be right back."

I stirred some creamer into the coffee and stared at the swirls as if they held some answers that I could give to my best friend.

"Where were we?" Rox asked a minute later as she reached for two coffee cups.

"We were talking about the wedding, but really, there's nothing happening on that front."

Setting the cups down, she leaned her elbows on the bar, her caramel hair brushing her jawline as she looked into my eyes. "Do you want to come to the house some night and talk about this? 'Cause, honey, it's time to move on so that something *can* happen. Don't you think?"

"Yes, of course. But..." I wouldn't know what to say.

"But, what?"

Craving its warmth, I wrapped my hands around my cup. "There's just a lot going on right now."

As if on cue, my phone dinged with a new text message. Retrieving it from my tote, I saw that it was from Heather. "Jeez Louise! You're not supposed to be speaking to me. That should include texting."

Rox craned her neck to see the name displayed on my phone. "Tell me that doesn't say Heather Beckett."

"I wish I could."

"What in the world is she texting you for?"

I hesitated to open her text to find out. "You heard about what happened, right? You know, to her *friend*?"

"Kevin Lovely?" Rox nodded while she filled the cups. "Yeah, I heard."

"She's taking it pretty hard."

"I imagine his wife and kids are taking it even harder, so excuse me if I don't have that much sympathy for her."

Heather had been *persona non grata* with Rox ever since she tried to steal Rox's boyfriend back in the ninth grade, so I wasn't surprised by her reaction.

"I know, but I get the impression that they were pretty close," I said, raising my voice so that Rox could hear me from where she was filling two tumblers at the soda dispenser.

"Is this first-hand information or the same gossip that's been making the rounds the last couple of months?" she asked.

"Apparently, I missed out on most of that gossip, but based on what I've heard since the accident happened, some of both."

"Both." Rox placed the tumblers on a plastic tray next to the coffee mugs and then rejoined me at the end of the bar. "Then that means that you've done more than just text with Heather."

"I ran into her on Saturday and we talked for a few minutes."

"Something tells me that there's a lot more to this story."

Since the classic rock Eddie's typically featured wasn't blasting through the overhead speakers, I looked over my shoulder to make sure we wouldn't be overheard. "Actually, Heather was waiting for Steve because she's convinced that her boyfriend's death wasn't accidental. But he wasn't there, so she had to make do with me."

Rox leaned on her elbows. "Oooh, we were just talking about this yesterday."

"About the accident?"

She nodded. "That it might not have been so accidental."

I assumed that this was more gossip that had made its way from Duke's to Eddie's. "What exactly have you heard?"

"Probably the same sort of stuff as you. You know, about Heather's predecessor and the tempers that had been flaring."

I didn't know a thing about the other women in Kevin Lovely's busy life beyond what Lucille had told me.

"Also the threats that her dad made," Rox added as if

it were common knowledge.

"What?!"

"You haven't heard about Scarlett's dad?"

Not only hadn't I heard about her dad, this was the first time I'd heard Scarlett's name mentioned. "This is all news to me."

"It was to me, too, before Sofia told me about how her cousin Scarlett had a thing for Kevin Lovely."

I turned to watch twenty-something Sofia deliver the drink order to Ernie Kozarek's table. "A thing like a little crush?"

"From what Sofia said, it wasn't so little. Scarlett was head over heels in love with the guy."

"And then what, he threw her over for Heather?"

"I'm not sure about the timing," Rox said as we both waved to Peggy Como and Sylvia Jeppesen, two of Gram's friends entering the bar. "But Sofia made it sound like Scarlett's father put an end to their relationship."

Ordinarily, I would have gone over to say hello to the two silver-haired ladies in matching pink bowling shirts, but I was much more interested in what else the perky brunette showing them to their table had to say. "Do you think Sofia would be willing to tell me what she told you?"

Rox's eyes widened. "You mean officially? Like you want to interview her?"

"No, no." I didn't want anyone to think that I was "officially" interviewing anyone connected to the death of Kevin Lovely, especially one of my friends who might happen to mention it to Steve. "Since Heather already managed to suck me into the Kevin Lovely relationship vortex, I'm just curious to hear what Sofia has to say about the guy."

"Just curious, huh?" Rox shot me a sly grin as she topped off my coffee. "I bet you are."

"It's the truth." At least as close to the truth as I was willing to get.

"Which, knowing you, means that you want to unofficially interview Sofia without anyone who carries a badge finding out about it."

"Something like that." Actually, exactly like that. "So please don't say anything to Steve."

"You can count on me." Rox dropped the grin. "But if you learn something that makes you think that Kevin Lovely's accident wasn't just an accident, *you'll* say something to Steve, right?"

"You know I'd have to." He wouldn't be happy to hear it, but if there were more to the story than a guy careening off the road to miss hitting something like a neighbor's cat, Steve would want to know.

Rox nodded. "Do you want to eat or talk first?"

"I can order something to go if you can spare her for a few minutes." I watched Sofia step behind the bar to fill two tumblers with ice water. "Maybe when she's done taking Sylvia and Peggy's order."

"It's slow right now, so I can handle that." Rox pointed at the table in the far corner, the one that would be farthest away from prying eyes and ears. "Take your coffee and I'll ask her to join you back there. What do you want to go? We have a ham and cheese calzone on special today."

That sounded a lot yummier than the chef's salad that I'd had in mind, so I wasted no time contemplating the extra calories I would be consuming. I had more intriguing things to think about. "Fine. No rush getting the order to the kitchen since I won't be leaving right away."

Plus, I didn't know how long I might have to wait for Sofia. But no sooner had I settled into the solid oak chair at the table than Sofia slid onto the seat opposite me.

Her dark, thick braid fell over her shoulder as she leaned close, providing me a glimpse of the enviable cleavage that was hiding under her black Eddie's Place T-shirt. "Roxanne said you wanted to talk to me about Kevin Lovely."

Sofia spoke in hushed tones, as if some reverence were required when speaking of the dead, even though the little sneer tugging at the corner of her mouth suggested that she didn't revere him in the slightest.

Cradling my coffee cup with my palms, I smiled as our eyes locked. "Not officially," I said because Sofia knew where I worked, and I didn't want her or anyone else thinking that we were doing anything beyond having a private chat. "Roxanne mentioned that you two thought that his death might not have been an accident, and that sounded so much like what someone else told me that I thought we should talk."

Sofia sat up straight, her chestnut brown eyes wide like a child whose hand had been caught in the cookie jar. "I don't really know anything."

I didn't believe that for a second. "Yeah, my friend doesn't know a lot about this either, but she has some strong opinions about how someone wanted Kevin Lovely dead."

Sofia stared into the depths of my coffee cup. "I didn't say anything like that. Not to Roxanne. Not to anybody."

"Okay, do you mind telling me what you did say?"

"I don't want to get anyone into trouble."

"You won't be. I'm just trying to help my friend and, if I'm being totally honest, me, because she won't stop bugging me about this."

Sofia lifted her gaze to meet mine. "You're talking about Heather Beckett, right?"

Were there no secrets in this town?

I nodded. "She's taking his death really hard."

"Yeah, my cousin is, too."

"Scarlett?" I asked, hoping that Sofia would assume that I knew as many of Port Merritt's dirty little secrets as she did.

Blowing out a breath, she leaned back in her chair. "Scarlett's a mess. She headed back to school Sunday. I didn't have to work, so I was at her house most of the day and saw her off. Scarlett couldn't stop crying. According to my aunt she'd been like that all weekend."

Okay. Now we were getting somewhere. "She must have really loved him."

Sofia's glossy mouth tightened. "Oh, she loved him something crazy. Probably always will."

"She knew he was married, right?"

"Oh, yeah. She worked with him and his wife."

"Holy cow!" Kevin Lovely was having an affair with this girl right under his wife's nose?

Sofia nodded. "Yeah. That's pretty much what I said when I found out."

"That they were sleeping together?"

"That Scarlett was pregnant."

Chapter Eleven

By the time I got back to my desk and did a brain dump to write down everything I had gleaned from Sofia, my calzone had become soggy from an hour cooling inside a takeout box, and I regretted not ordering that salad.

But what I had in front of me, instead of a super-satisfying lunch, was enough dirt on Kevin Lovely to satisfy my curiosity about the kind of man Heather had hooked up with.

However, knowing that the handsome guy smiling in that family photo I had seen hadn't been as devoted to his family as he might have been when that picture was taken didn't mean that anyone killed him.

As both Steve and Ben would be quick to remind me, Kevin Lovely died from injuries he sustained from a single-car accident. With his own son as an eyewitness, we knew that no one forced him off the road and no one had been with him inside the vehicle.

So, if no one else was around at the time of the accident, it didn't matter that Scarlett's father had threatened to punch her baby daddy's lights out for taking advantage of his daughter.

Plus, that had happened almost four months ago.

In the meantime, Kevin had moved on with Heather.

Scarlett had even moved on once she came to realize that Kevin wasn't going to leave his wife for her.

As Sofia explained to me shortly after she joined me at the table, "My cousin did something really dumb, but she isn't stupid."

I kept my mouth shut and took notes while Sofia did the talking for most of the next ten minutes.

"According to my mom, her sister hasn't stopped blaming herself for asking Veronica to hire Scarlett. It was just supposed to be a summer job while she was home from college."

I asked if the two women were close friends.

"Not anymore!" Sofia had stated without an ounce of humor. She then went on to confide how her cousin had been embarrassed that her parents confronted the Lovelys the night they found out she was pregnant.

I underlined the words *confronted them that night* and stared at them for several seconds.

If Scarlett's parents had both said their piece back in July, why would either of them want to confront Kevin Lovely again?

When the fall quarter began, Scarlett had gone back to college up north in Bellingham, so it wasn't like her parents needed to take any action to separate her from the man she thought she loved.

Sofia truly believed that they had wanted nothing to do with the guy and that Veronica was the one who would have wanted to take her anger out on her cheat of a husband.

I made a note of the approximate date that Veronica would have found out that her husband was cheating on her with the daughter of one of her best friends.

And Veronica had been the one to throw them together day after day, which should have made it all the more infuriating.

Based on everything I had pieced together the last few days, Veronica Lovely would have had some solid motivation to get rid of her husband.

If Frankie Rickard, the county prosecutor/coroner, had found Kevin Lovely's cause of death the least bit suspicious and had wanted Steve to do a more thorough investigation before she signed the death certificate, I would have marched to her office to tell her everything I'd learned about our victim and the people in his life.

But she didn't. And the death certificate was already a done deal.

So, other than finding someone else who shared Heather's suspicions, I didn't see much use for the notes I had spent most of the last hour scribbling, and I tossed my legal pad in my desk drawer.

That's when I noticed Karla Tate, Frankie's death investigation coordinator and the lead of the five administrative assistants who sat down the hall from me, glancing in my direction while talking to someone on the phone.

My stomach clenched with the certainty that I was the subject of that conversation.

The congealed grease I had just consumed probably contributed to my distress, but I didn't need to make matters worse by not getting back to doing the work I was being paid for.

That included keeping all the prosecuting attorneys and their staff highly caffeinated, but as I headed for the breakroom to make a fresh pot of coffee, I heard Karla call my name.

Uh-oh.

"I have a project for you if you have time," she said at the same time the cell phone in my trousers pocket started ringing.

"Sorry." I smiled apologetically. "Let me get this and I'll be right back."

Pulling out my phone, I saw Heather's number.

Crap! I had become so engrossed while talking to Sofia I had forgotten all about Heather's text.

"Sorry." Not really, but I thought it would help diffuse whatever new accusations she intended to blast into my eardrum. "I got caught up with work and wasn't able to get back to you."

"Is that where you are?" Heather asked after an awkward pause. "At work?"

Why wouldn't I be? "Yep."

"I need to see you before you go."

I wasn't following her. "Before I leave for the day?"

She heaved a sigh as if I were testing her patience. "Before you leave town."

Seriously? This stupid rumor had made its way to Heather?

I dropped into my desk chair. "I'm not leaving town anytime soon." Although the prospect of getting out of Dodge was becoming more appealing by the second.

"Oh, I thought I'd heard something about you and Steve—"

"It's just somebody's idea of a bad joke, and I really need to get back to work." Because Jan had joined Karla at her desk, and now she was looking at me and shaking her head.

My heart started beating double-time because they clearly knew something that I didn't.

And by the huddle my two favorite administrative assistants were in, it didn't look like a good something.

Was I about to get fired for taking one too many long lunches?

"I'm at work, too," Heather said, her voice so low I could barely hear her over the pounding of my pulse in my ear. "Can you meet me at the dog park at six? You still go there most nights with your dog, right?"

I'd seen her and her son there a few times with their Irish setter, but we'd always managed to avoid speaking to one another.

Okay, I had avoided Heather just like I had been avoiding her ever since I moved back to Port Merritt. And she hadn't seemed to have minded in the slightest because I'd seen her do the exact same thing when she made an abrupt about-face in the cereal aisle last month at the Red Apple Market.

But that was before her boyfriend died, and I woke up in this Twilight Zone parallel universe where she actually wanted to talk to me.

That didn't mean I wanted to talk to her, but now wasn't the time to debate the matter.

Especially with Jan and Karla walking toward me with such somber expressions they could have been headed to a friend's funeral.

I just hoped it wasn't mine!

"Yes. Fine, see you at six." I quickly ended the call, tossed my cell phone onto the stack of manila folders that should have been filed hours earlier, and pasted a smile on my face.

"Sorry about that." And this time I meant it.

Focusing my attention on Karla, I tried to not stare at the tension tightening the creases that the last four decades of smoking had carved into her upper lip. "Is there something that you wanted some help with?"

"Actually..." Karla lowered her voice even though it was rare for anyone to venture back into the windowless bowels of the third floor. "Frankie asked me to do something."

Based on the weight of the dread hunching the sixty-year-old's shoulders and the flush igniting Jan's cheeks, this wasn't going to be good. "What?"

Karla grimaced. "I'm supposed to get you to the breakroom for a surprise party."

Oh, no.

If this was what I thought it was, this was beyond not good. "Please tell me it's somebody's birthday."

"Frankie heard that you and Steve were eloping and wanted to give you a little send-off," Karla said. "I reminded her that a bunch of us went to your bridal shower, but you know how she is. She likes to celebrate happy news."

I groaned. "I know, but we're not—"

"I knew it!" Karla looked to Jan. "I told you she would've said something if the rumor was true."

Jan took a nervous glance over her shoulder at the sound of footfalls in the hall. "That doesn't change the fact that Frankie sent me to Duke's to buy cupcakes, and there are people heading to the breakroom right now."

Criminy, I needed to get out of the Twilight Zone!

Chapter Twelve

Four hours after Frankie turned our department "meeting" into a holiday kickoff party, where I did my best to laugh off the rumor about my impending nuptials, I was standing at the entrance of the dog park with Fozzie when Steve called.

"Is there something I should know?" he asked.

About why Heather wanted to meet me here?

I could guess at the reason, and that was the last thing I wanted to discuss with him. "No. Why?"

"Wanda was acting funny around me most of the afternoon."

Wanda was the chief of police's secretary—a no-nonsense mother hen who ruled the roost at the station.

She was also someone who could rival Lucille when it came to having her ear to the ground, so I had a bad feeling about what was coming. Doubly so since I could see Heather walking her Irish setter in my direction. "Funny ha-ha, or funny weird?"

"Weird, like she had a secret I wasn't in on. Finally, she asked me where we were getting married. Renee

Ireland asked the same thing when I passed her on the street. Even suggested that you write something up after we get back, and she'll get our wedding announcement in the paper."

Good grief. "You set her straight and told her we hadn't even set a date yet, right?" Because Renee was the closest thing Port Merritt had to an investigative reporter, and I didn't want to see our names in next week's *Gazette.*

"Yeah, but what's going on?"

"Someone made a joke about us eloping, and I guess a few people took it seriously."

"Do I need to set someone else straight?"

I assumed he meant Lucille. "Already taken care of," I said over the full-throated commotion Fozzie was making as Heather and her dog rounded the corner into the park.

"Good. I'd hate to think that it was such a slow news day that this is what everybody was talking about. I mean, come on."

While Fozzie barked and strained at the leash to get closer to the setter, I raised a finger to ask that her unsmiling owner give me a minute. "No kidding."

"What's got Cujo all riled up?" Steve asked.

"It's just someone at the park he doesn't know." And could probably sense that she was no friend.

"You heading back home soon?"

I couldn't imagine that Heather had anything to say to me that would take more than twenty minutes. "Yep. Want to meet me there around six-thirty?"

Steve had another call, which allowed me to pocket my phone before Heather started giving me the death stare.

"Sorry," I said to Heather while I stroked Fozzie's head with my free hand to calm him. "My guard dog here thinks he needs to sound ferocious when he meets someone new."

Closing the distance between us, Heather offered Fozzie her hand so that he could sniff it. "He just needs to know that I'm no threat. Neither is Ginger."

I had no doubt that was true of the four-legged beauty wagging her tail. I wasn't so sure about the two-legged one standing next to her.

I also didn't have time to overthink the situation because a gangly teenaged boy running past us with a big shepherd mix had Fozzie growling as if he were ready to rumble.

Pointing to the dirt trail that bordered the tree-lined park, I pulled Fozzie close and started walking. "Let's get away from other people or he'll never settle down."

Plus, I had a date with a hot cop, and I wanted to get this meeting over with.

Heather fell into step by my side and, smartly, gave Ginger ten feet of leash to create some separation between the two dogs.

"I wanted to apologize for how I acted on the phone last night," she finally said when I stopped to let Fozzie water the base of a young cedar tree near a wooden bench.

Heather couldn't have surprised me more if she had

reared back and punched me in the nose.

"You were upset. I knew that and didn't take it personally." Yes, I was lying. I'd always taken everything she'd done very personally.

"You're just being nice."

I didn't know what to say to that because she was absolutely right. "I'm not *that* nice."

"Yes, you are. You wouldn't have agreed to help me otherwise, not after... Well, let's just say I haven't been nearly as nice to you."

What was happening?

Was Heather dishing out all this sugar because she was still holding out hope that there was some dirt on Veronica Lovely that I could unearth? "I don't think there's anything else I can do if that's where this is going."

Heather's face hardened, her perfect skin gleaming like alabaster in the glow from a nearby streetlight. "Can't you just accept an apology without assuming that I have an ulterior motive?"

I could if this were Steve, Gram, or Rox, the three people I trusted most in the world. But this was Heather Carver Beckett, who had shown no inclination to be anything beyond barely civil to me in the two and a half years since I moved back to Port Merritt.

There had to be an ulterior motive to why she had wanted to meet here, but I slapped a smile on my face as if that were a thought I wouldn't dream of entertaining.

"Of course. Apology accepted. I hope there are no hard feelings," I said, echoing the same crapola I'd told her twenty-five years ago in the vice principal's office.

She stood in silence for several seconds as if she were contemplating actually believing me this time.

With biting wind gusts that made fallen pine needles and rust-colored leaves dance across the trail, I raised the hood of my jacket and wished I'd changed into something warmer.

"Want to walk to the half-mile marker?" Because even my dog was looking back at me as if to ask why we were just standing around, getting cold, when there was a perfectly good trail to walk. Plus, his favorite play area in the park was up ahead.

"Sure," Heather said, letting Ginger lead the way.

After a minute of nothing but the sounds of the cars passing by on L Street and the squeals of laughter from children having a lot more fun than I was, I'd had enough of contemplative Heather.

It was time for her to come clean about why she *had* to see me tonight.

"Is there anything else you wanted to talk about?" There had to have been because she could have apologized via text. Or, better yet, she could have opted to never contact me again, which would feel much more normal than this bizarre frenemy thing we'd been doing ever since the moment she stepped into my grandmother's house.

"There is one thing," Heather said.

Of course there was.

She appeared to be waiting for two preschoolers to run toward us with their mom and a floppy-eared little mutt.

They were regulars in the park, so the kids raced to pet my bear of a dog—attention Fozzie was always happy to stop for. But once the mom and I exchanged quick hellos and they left to head for the exit, I pointed to the sign marking the exercise area where our dogs could run around off-leash. "Let's let them play while we talk."

There were no other dogs or humans within sight, so I didn't hesitate to unhook the leash to let Fozzie go have some fun.

At least one of us would, I thought as I turned to Heather.

But instead of letting Ginger run free, Heather pulled the setter to her side as if she were a therapy dog and removed a thin, white envelope from a pocket of her navy stadium jacket. "Would you give this to Steve?"

If I went home and handed Steve that envelope, it would be as good as admitting that I hadn't wanted him to know that I was standing next to her when he called. I'd already had an aggravating day and saw no reason to pile on more aggravation from his old girlfriend.

"You should do that yourself," I said, keeping my hands to myself.

"He doesn't want to hear from me. He's made that very clear by not taking any of my calls."

Then that should have given her a clue about how well the contents of that envelope would be received.

Still, if Heather was determined to use a go-between, she had a better, more official option. "You could drop it off at the police station. Just hand it to Wanda and she'll make sure he gets it."

And leave me out of it.

Fozzie barked, springing toward us out of a crouch and then dashing behind the trunk of a huge hemlock as if to beg us to come play with him.

Whining, Ginger tugged at her leash to join him, but after a couple of attempts only succeeded in wrapping herself around my legs.

I reached for the leash to avoid getting tripped if Ginger decided to make any sudden moves, but it was her owner I should have been more concerned about because she took that opportunity to slap that white envelope in my hand.

"Hey! You can't just stick me with this," I said, alarmed to see Heather backing away from me with her Irish setter. "You need to deliver this yourself."

She started walking toward the trail. "I'm done wasting time. You're going to see Steve tonight, so just give it to him then."

No, no. Heather, of all people, was not going to put me in this ridiculous position with Steve.

"You can't seriously expect me to do this," I yelled at her backside.

She looked over her shoulder. "If you care about getting to the truth as much as you always said you do, you'll give that to him."

"That is so not fair!"

After giving me a dismissive wave that felt more like a one-fingered salute, the girl that I once thought would be my best friend forever kept walking.

"Heather!" I called after her, but there was no response as she disappeared in the shadows between the streetlights. Only Fozzie came running as if he were ready to go home and get some loving from the very nice human who would be waiting for us there.

After the day I'd had, I could use some loving, too.

I frowned at the envelope in my hand. "Loving first. Then I'll give him this later."

Preferably much later.

Chapter Thirteen

Dropping his fork to his dinner plate, Steve turned to me. "Okay, what's wrong?"

"It's just been a long, strange day," I said, toying with one of the meatballs in front of me to avoid making eye contact.

"You've hardly said a word to me since you got back from the park."

"Sure, I have. I asked you what you wanted for dinner. And then you responded with one word: spaghetti. So, which one of us is the one specializing in brevity tonight?"

"Didn't think I needed to expound on my answer. But you do," he gently said. "Something's bothering you. It's the only time you're this quiet. Plus, you're not eating."

My stomach was so full with nervous knots, I didn't have room for anything else.

"The cupcake I had at work must have spoiled my appetite." I stabbed the meatball and fed it to the dog that had been sitting between us for the last fifteen minutes.

"Uh-huh." Steve leaned back in his chair.

I pointed my licked-clean fork at him. "You could at least pretend to believe me."

"I could." His dark eyes softened like melting chocolate. "But I like not having to pretend with you."

Dang. He knew exactly what to say to make me melt. And if a dog hadn't been blocking my path, I would have jumped him on the spot.

Instead, I put down the fork and reached for Steve's hand. "I could get used to you saying things like that."

His lips curled as his warm palm pressed against mine. "Stick around. Maybe for the rest of your life."

"That's the plan."

"It's a good plan."

"I think so, too," I said, grateful that this guy loved me when the thought had seemed unimaginable when we first started dating.

Steve dropped the smile. "You're not worrying because of all this wedding talk."

"What? No, I'm not worried at all." While I knew that wasn't entirely believable, I'd said as much as I'd wanted to about our wedding for one day, so I hoped he'd give me a pass.

Skepticism creased his brow. "If it's not the wedding, what is it?"

I reached into my jeans pocket and pulled out the envelope that I'd been dreading giving him.

"Don't shoot the messenger," I said, setting it on the table so that he could see that it was addressed to him.

Steve frowned. "What's this?"

"I'm pretty sure it's not a love letter from your former

girlfriend. That would just be too weird considering the circumstances."

"This is from Heather?"

"Yep."

He turned his frown on me. "Then what's weird is the fact that you're acting as her messenger."

I couldn't argue with that. "Trust me, it wasn't my idea."

"I take it she called you again."

"It appears I'm not worthy of the silent treatment just yet."

Tapping his index finger against the table, Steve stared at the envelope.

"Are you going to open that or just glare at it?" Because I was dying to know what Heather had to say.

The tapping stopped. "Pretty sure I already know what's in it."

But I didn't. "Will you please just open it?"

"Why? Is the suspense killing you?"

Yes!

I shrugged. "It could be something important having to do with your investigation."

"Uh-huh," he muttered while tearing open the envelope.

Steve unfolded the single sheet of white paper, sitting like a poker player holding his cards close to his vest so that I couldn't see what he was reading. Then, he refolded the page and stuffed it into the front pocket of his blue jeans.

"Well?" I asked when he offered me no explanation

beyond an amused look.

"You were right."

Because Heather really had some new information for him? "About what specifically?"

"It wasn't a love letter."

"Really?" I scowled at him. "That's all you're going to tell me?"

Rising from the table, Steve stepped around Fozzie to plant a quick kiss on my lips. "That's all I've got for you, Chow Mein."

While I had never minded the nickname he bestowed upon me back in the third grade, I hated being kept in the dark, especially where Heather was concerned.

"You're a jerk," I grumbled.

He grinned. "I love you, too."

Late Wednesday morning, I was sitting at my desk, combing through the social media history of one of the defendants coming to trial after the holidays. Not that I had expected him to post anything incriminating. It was just one of the many routine background checks I ran on an almost daily basis.

If I found anything the least bit revelatory about the person, I was supposed to copy it into a document to be reviewed by a paralegal. From there, if the information was flagged for further review, it would go up the chain to the attorney prosecuting the case.

After over two hours, the only thing I'd managed to find that seemed related to the charge of robbery in the second degree, namely the car that Zack Wooten had stolen after a night of partying, was a photo of him looking wasted with his co-defendant. It wasn't listed as having been uploaded the same night that they boosted the car. But after I saw that Zack had posted it the previous Saturday, the pattern of partying together seemed strong enough for me to add that photo and all the others posted within a three-week period to my document. It was a long shot that there would be any new witnesses to be interviewed in those photos, but if there were, I did my best to provide names to go along with the faces.

One of those pictures featured the defendant at a table with a group of friends with their glasses raised in a toast. The caption read, "Happy birthday, Zack." Five out of the six people sharing his table had been tagged with their social media profile names, making my job all the easier.

One of the names was Scarlett Fortenberry, which caused me to reach for the legal pad in my desk drawer to make a note of her last name.

I wasn't sure that this Scarlett was Sofia's cousin, but her coloring was certainly similar to Sofia's and she definitely appeared to be around twenty-one.

But the older guy sitting next to her, putting his hand up like he didn't want his picture taken, was what caused my heart to pound with certainty.

Because the sixth person at the table was Kevin Lovely.

Chapter Fourteen

Sofia didn't look happy when I stepped into Eddie's Place an hour later.

I knew that it wasn't my mere presence two days in a row that caused her to make a sour face. That didn't happen until I asked to speak with her in private.

Then, Sofia heaved a sigh that rivaled my mother's at her most put-upon.

I couldn't blame her. Most of the tables were occupied with hungry patrons here on their lunch hour, and she didn't have time to converse about anything other than what was on the menu. Which was exactly what Rox was communicating with a cocked head as she watched us from behind the bar.

"It'll have to be fast and in the kitchen," Sofia told me, leading the way at a brisk pace.

I turned to Rox as I dashed past. "I swear I'll make it quick."

"You'd better," she yelled after me. "And if you keep showing up here, I'm gonna put you to work."

Nice threat, but since I often filled in for her or Eddie

on the weekends they needed to be home with their baby, it was an empty one and we both knew it.

Still, I was all too aware that I wasn't especially welcome this noon hour—a fact that Sofia made painfully obvious once the kitchen door closed behind my back.

"I've already told you more than I should have," she said, an edge to her voice that made her sound nervous. Her eyes darted toward Carlos, the cook getting her next order ready while he sang along with the Foo Fighters hit blasting from his radio.

Even though Carlos seemed oblivious to our presence, Sofia lowered her volume to almost a whisper. "My cousin will *not* be happy if it gets back to her that I'm talking to you."

"She won't hear it from me." But I was more concerned about the not-so-happy cousin in front of me. "Has something happened since we talked that I should know about?"

Looking down at her zebra-striped sneakers, she clamped her mouth shut and shook her head.

That would be a yes.

"Did someone say something to you about talking to me?" I couldn't imagine that any of the oldsters who saw us sitting together yesterday would have said anything to make Sofia uncomfortable, and I was quite sure that Rox wouldn't have. Had someone else seen us together?

"Not specifically." Sofia picked up a pair of tongs and added a generous helping of greens to a salad plate. "But I had dinner with my parents last night and happened to mention that questions were being asked about Kevin

Lovely's death."

"That shouldn't have come as any surprise considering the circumstances."

Sofia focused on the bleu cheese dressing she was ladling over the salad. "That's what I thought before my mom informed me that we weren't going to talk about that."

"She didn't want to talk about that during dinner?" Easily understandable since Gram didn't like me talking shop at the table.

"The family isn't going to talk about this, period." Sofia shot me a cool glance as she took five long strides to pick up the chopped salad Carlos had set next to a steaming hot pizza. "So, whatever you're here to ask, I guess I'm supposed to say 'no comment.'"

"Huh?" Carlos asked, turning to her as she headed for the door. Then he gave me a friendly chin salute. "Hey, Char. You back for another calzone?"

If I ever wanted to fit into my wedding dress again, I needed to lay off my favorite food group: cheesy carbs.

"It was delicious." Or would have been if I had eaten it when it was still hot. "But I need something a little lighter, so let's make it a chicken Caesar salad to go," I said, taking an order ticket from the counter to write it down for him.

I also needed one more minute alone with Sofia before she completely clammed up on me, so I grabbed the pizza platter, a short stack of plastic plates, and bumped the kitchen door open with my hip just like I had countless times while Rox was on maternity leave.

Only this time no one had asked for my help, and by the grimace on Sofia's face as I approached, she clearly didn't appreciate the assistance.

"Where?" I asked.

"Table four. And I already told you, *no comment.* So you can go sit at the bar and talk to Roxanne if you feel compelled to talk with someone."

I gave Sofia what I hoped was a reassuring smile. "I know. I just want to show you something."

She jutted her jaw defiantly, but her dark eyes sharpened with interest.

Despite her best intentions to toe the family line, I could tell she was intrigued.

Which was enough for me to work with.

"I'll deliver this to table four and make sure they have everything they need. You do what you need to do out here, then meet me back in the kitchen." Then, before Sofia could protest, I headed to the table occupied by two salesmen I recognized from a nearby car dealership.

After I topped off their coffee cups, I returned the carafe to the warmer behind the bar and was just about to dash back into the kitchen when Rox blocked my path.

She narrowed her eyes. "What are you up to?"

"I'm just pitching in while Carlos makes me a salad."

Suspicion tugged at a corner of her mouth. "I'll tell you what else you're doing. You're making my server nervous, so whatever is going on I want it to stop. Because Eddie and I like her, and we don't want her to quit because one of our friends is hassling her."

"I'm not hassling her," I said, laughing off the accusation.

Rox planted her hands at her slender hips. "Uh-huh."

"Okay. I'm not *intentionally* hassling her. I just need her to help me with one little thing and then I'll go."

"This is because of her cousin's connection to Kevin Lovely, isn't it," Rox said in my ear while Joan Jett's "Bad Reputation" blasted above our heads.

I nodded. "I'm just trying to get some facts straight."

For Heather. Kind of. But mainly because the more I found out about Kevin Lovely's life, the more intrigued I became by his death.

The person I thought might be able to help me with those facts was walking toward the kitchen with the dirty dishes from the table she'd just cleared, so I set my feet in motion. "Gotta go."

Rox wrapped her hand around my arm before I could make a clean getaway. "It *was* an accident, right?"

"Absolutely," I said with as much conviction as I could muster. "That's what Steve said."

"Then how come you don't sound like you believe him?"

Good question, and not one that I could answer because I was certain that he hadn't lied to me. Steve was hard for me to read—something he prided himself in. But still, I was as certain about this as I could be.

And anyway, why would he lie?

I couldn't answer that question either.

Chapter Fifteen

"Okay, what's wrong?" Gram asked when she caught me staring down at the pot of turkey gravy bubbling on her stove instead of stirring it as she had instructed.

I didn't want to talk about trying to squeeze out information from Sofia. She could confirm that the fresh-faced brunette sitting next to Kevin Lovely was her cousin Scarlett, but other than that, Sofia appeared to be as curious about why they would be sitting with Zack Wooten as I was.

For good reason.

As Sofia put it, "Scarlett was crazy about Zack back in high school, but she dumped his sorry ass two years ago."

I could almost hear Steve's voice in my head. "So they all knew one another. So what?"

What are you trying to prove?

That it seemed weird that these former high school sweethearts were having a reunion with her current lover as onlooker?

That Heather was right?

That there was more to the story of how Kevin Lovely died?

It sure felt that way while I watched Steve read her note to him.

And yet I had never sensed that he had lied to me about his investigation.

Withheld information, yes. There was nothing unusual about that. But lied? No.

What then?

What the heck was the purpose of all the wheel spinning I had been doing? Did I really think that I owed anything to Heather after all these years?

"Darned if I know," I muttered under my breath while I stirred.

Gram touched the sleeve of my olive tunic sweater, giving me a nudge so that she could open the oven. "What, honey?"

"Nothing." With Steve expected to arrive any minute for our weekly dinner date with my grandmother, absolutely, positively nothing I wanted to discuss.

"Well, something's obviously bothering you."

"It's just been a long, weird week," I said, paraphrasing what I had told Steve during last night's dinner.

Gram frowned as she removed the aluminum foil cover from a casserole dish of stuffing. "It's only Wednesday."

"Then it only feels like a long, weird week."

She closed the oven and then took the whisk from me to stir the gravy. "What's so weird about it? Other than the fact that you and Stevie were supposed to elope yesterday."

"There was that." Definitely something that should register on any family member's weirdometer and it had the added benefit of having nothing to do with Kevin Lovely's death.

"Oh, I can tell you why it feels like it's been such a weird week." She nodded with all the self-assurance of someone who was typically right. "It's because of that strange encounter you had with Heather Carver."

"Beckett."

She wrinkled her nose. "Whatever."

"And let's not mention her again tonight. Since she's Steve's old girlfriend, there's no need to—"

"Don't tell me that he doesn't know that the two of you 'chatted' last Saturday."

"He knows."

"I get the sense you're holding something back. So he knows *all* about that?" Gram asked, peering at me over her trifocals.

The look of doubt penetrating my eye sockets would have been all she needed to extract a full confession from me back when Heather was still my BFF.

Fortunately, that was then. "Pretty much."

"Pretty much doesn't sound like a yes."

Buckling under the intensity of her scrutiny, I decided that this would be a good time to bury my nose in the weekly *Gazette* she had been reading at her kitchen table. "I didn't bore him with all the details."

Gram scoffed. "Well, that can only mean one thing, given how you insisted on driving your mother to meet with Veronica Lovely. Heather managed to convince you that the woman had something to do with her husband's death."

While I tried to come up with a plausible denial, my focus shifted to Kevin Lovely's picture at the top of page eight.

I did a quick scan of the information provided for his obituary, which wasn't much.

Date of birth, date of death, surviving family members, and then it closed with a line that didn't surprise me in the slightest: *Private memorial services will be held at a future date.*

The last people Veronica would want to see at her husband's funeral would be the other women in his life.

Curious onlookers like me wouldn't be welcome either. Dang it.

"Charmaine, are you listening to me?" Gram abruptly asked.

I turned back to her. "Sure. I was just—"

She held up a hand to stop me. "I knew it had to be Heather's influence when you came up with that flimsy excuse to look at those emails on your mother's phone."

"I just wanted—"

"Oh, I know what you wanted. You wanted to see if you could catch Veronica Lovely lying about the night her husband died."

There was no denying it. "I was just trying to help. Besides, we wouldn't want Mom to get involved with—"

"Don't even try to make this sound like you were doing this for your mother."

"But if Heather and some other people in town are right, and there's something suspicious about the way Kevin Lovely died—"

"You need to stop talking to Lucille," Gram said on a sigh while the door behind her swung open, and the woman I least wanted to see at that moment flashed me a bright smile. "I swear she has Alice half-convinced the man was murdered."

Marietta gaped at her mother. "Who was murdered?"

Gasping, Gram pressed her hand to her heart. "Don't sneak up on me like that."

"Sorry. I wasn't trying to be sneaky." My mother inched closer in a pair of chunky, low-heeled ankle boots that gave her an après-ski look with the snowflake sweater and black leggings she was wearing. "You weren't talking about Kevin Lovely, were you?"

"We were just talking about..." Gram shot me a glance as if she wanted to pass this hot potato.

And I said the first thing that popped into my head. "About how Lucille watches too many cop shows on TV."

Marietta's eyes widened. "That may be, but were you saying that she thinks Kevin Lovely was murdered?"

"She thinks that everyone who doesn't die at the ripe old age of one hundred and two could have been murdered." And with that non-answer hanging between us much like the fog outside, it was time to change the subject before anyone else stepped through that door. Namely Steve.

Stepping away from the table, I pointed at the middle of the three big snowflakes stretched across my mother's spectacular chest. "Cute sweater." I looked past her, out the back door window, at the shiny new silver Mercedes SUV dwarfing my Subaru in Gram's driveway.

Since Barry typically dropped her off when he had other plans after work on Wednesday, I had expected to see him behind the wheel of the new car they had purchased as an early Christmas present to themselves. Instead, the Mercedes was unoccupied.

When I looked back at my mother, the corners of her green eyes lifted with pride.

"You're here by yourself?" I asked her.

Her strawberry-painted lips curled with an equal measure of pleasure. "Barry had practice, so I thought I'd take my new ride out for a spin."

Gram tsked. "In the dark? Don't get me wrong. I'm always happy to see you, but I hate thinking of you driving at night."

"Plus, it's foggy out," I added, perfectly aware that I was piling on, but at least we weren't talking about Kevin Lovely anymore.

Marietta pursed her mouth. "It's not that foggy and I can see in the dark just fine, thank you very much."

Only because she had recently acquired some prescription glasses.

She sniffed the air like Fozzie did when we passed his favorite hamburger stand. "What's that heavenly smell?"

"I have a turkey in the oven." Gram went back to stirring the gravy. "Have you eaten, honey?"

"No," Marietta said. "But you're having turkey? Like a second Thanksgiving dinner?"

That's exactly what it was. This time, cooked the way I liked it, which was why I had requested it for tonight when Steve and I drove Gram home last Thursday.

And as a bonus it wouldn't make anyone sick.

"Yes, and we're having the green bean casserole you like," Gram said as if she needed to sweeten the pot.

"Oh, I do like that, but you don't have to feed me, Mama." Marietta eyed the large pot of mashed potatoes next to the gravy. "Unless you're sure you have enough."

"Of course there's enough." Gram winked at me. "I always make sure that there's enough for one more."

Only because my mother had a habit of showing up around dinnertime whenever Barry wasn't home to cook for her. Which made me wonder what was going on tonight.

"What kind of practice is Barry at?" I asked.

Marietta gave her head a little shake. "Basketball. A friend of his talked him into helping as an assistant coach this season."

I remembered him coaching the team back when I was in high school. "I didn't realize that he was doing that again. Varsity or JV?"

She blinked. "JV?"

Had my mother forgotten everything about high school athletics? "Junior varsity."

"Oh. No, Barry said middle school. Specifically, the seventh-grade boys," she added, slinging her tote bag over the nearest kitchen chair.

What?

I stared as she took a seat. "He's coaching the *local*

seventh-grade boys' basketball team?"

"I believe he said he's the second assistant coach, whatever that means."

"Of the Hagen Middle School basketball team?" I asked to make sure. "The school that I went to." And the team that Jonah played for.

"I went there too. And now Barry's coaching there." Smiling contentedly, Marietta waved her hand with dramatic flair. "Our family legacy at Hagen continues."

"Hopefully, that will be fun for him," Gram chimed in as she brought us each a glass of white wine.

"You know what would be fun," I said, seizing this opportunity before Steve stepped through the door. "We should go to a game. I hear there's one this Friday." And I would bet dollars to doughnuts that Veronica Lovely would be there to cheer her son on.

It would be the perfectly normal thing to do—what a loving mom would do to help her son experience some sense of continuity after the sudden loss of his dad. And I wanted to see if there were any cracks in how "normally" this new widow acted in public.

Marietta fiddled with the stem of her glass. "I don't know. I wouldn't want my presence to distract from the game."

"Mom, it's not like anyone's going to rush across the court to ask for your autograph."

Her mouth flat-lined. "I'll have you know that I often get stopped at the store or beauty parlor by someone who wants an autograph."

Maybe by some middle schooler's grandma the first

few times she was spotted in town, but now that she'd been a Port Merritt resident for over a year, a Marietta Moreau sighting wasn't such a novelty anymore.

"Of course, if you're concerned about being a distraction in such a public setting, I understand," I said, trying a more conciliatory approach. "Gram and I will have to go and support Barry and the team without you."

My grandmother knitted her brows. "We will?"

"Unless you have a mahjong game that night." Which typically occupied her Friday evenings.

"We're on hiatus until after the holidays," Gram muttered unenthusiastically.

"It's a date then." Setting my wineglass on the table, I retrieved my phone from my tote. "I'll find out when we need to be there."

"I suppose I could wear something inconspicuous to avoid people making a fuss," Marietta said while inspecting her perfectly manicured nails. "Because if you're going, how would it look if I didn't attend my own husband's game?"

I knew my mother wouldn't be able to stomach the idea of sitting home alone while we went on a "date" without her.

"Let's make it our secret, though," she added with a coy curve to her lips. "I want to see the surprised expression on Barry's face when he sees us in the stands. So not a word to Steve during dinner."

I smiled while I searched for the game time. "He definitely won't hear about it from me."

Chapter Sixteen

"That was bizarre," Steve said, standing over a sudsy sink of dishes two hours later. "And not just because your mother kept apologizing about Thanksgiving."

"She still feels awful about giving you food poisoning, but beyond that, what was so bizarre? Dinner was great."

Steve handed me a plate to dry. "How about the fact that she didn't mention the wedding. Not once."

I didn't call that bizarre. I called that a blessing.

"I'm sure she's gotten the hint that she'll be the first to know when we're ready to make an announcement." Especially since that was what I'd been telling my mother every time she brought up the subject.

"And when do you think that will be?" Steve asked as he scrubbed a crusty casserole dish.

Even though his focus was on the task before him, I stepped aside to return the plate to the cupboard so he wouldn't see me struggling to come up with a witty response. "I don't know," I finally said, knowing my words were woefully inadequate and totally devoid of wit.

By the time I turned back to him, Steve was leaning

against the sink, his dark eyes boring into mine.

My mouth went dry.

I needed to say more.

He deserved more.

Say something.

Anything!

But my voice caught on the jumble of emotions clogging my throat.

"Maybe we should talk about this," he offered after several awkward seconds ticked by.

I nodded. "Not here." And please, not now.

I needed more time.

I wasn't sure why, but the ache in my heart told me that I needed it.

"No, not here. When you're ready," Steve added as if reading my mind.

My brain may have rendered me incapable of stringing words together to express my feelings, but my body knew exactly what to do. I rushed to him in two long strides, wrapped my arms around his neck, and kissed him, sweetly at first and then the kiss deepened while he held me tight.

"Oops!" Gram said as she entered the kitchen. "So sorry to interrupt."

I immediately pushed Steve away, my cheeks ablaze just like the rest of me. "You're not interrupting anything. We were just—"

"Oh, honey." Gram slowly shook her head. "Don't even bother because I know exactly what you were doing."

Fine. I didn't know what to say to that either.

"I just came in to put the kettle on," Gram said, picking it up. "Would either of you care for some tea?"

"Not me." I was already on the verge of breaking into a sweat and didn't need anything hot to push me over the edge.

I looked at Steve to let him answer for himself.

"No, thank you." He leaned close to whisper in my ear. "I want something else."

I elbowed him in the ribs while Gram filled the kettle at the sink.

"Okay, carry on," she said as she scurried back to the living room.

Steve didn't hesitate to sweep me into his arms. "You heard the woman."

"Hey!" I pressed back against his solid chest. "She's going to be back in two minutes tops, so don't start something you can't finish."

He took my hand—the one sporting the engagement ring he'd placed on it five months earlier—and brought my palm to his lips. "Trust me. We're gonna finish this."

"Is that a threat or a promise?" I teased.

"Yes."

Goody.

"Are we late?" my mother asked me on Friday as we followed Gram into the Hagen Middle School gymnasium. "It sounds like the game is already in progress."

From all the basketballs the two seventh-grade teams

were bouncing during their pre-game warm-up, it sounded like several games were in progress.

"We're not late," I assured Marietta, giving her a gentle nudge to keep pace with Gram. "They're warming up now. The game doesn't start until six-thirty."

Marietta swung around and leveled a glare at me. "You said we needed to leave the house no later than five-thirty if we wanted to get good seats."

I lied.

But I knew my mother.

When Gram and I promptly arrived at five-twenty-five, Marietta called us upstairs to solicit our opinions about the outfit she'd selected: a black quilted vest to wear over the saffron cashmere turtleneck I'd given her for Christmas two years ago, and a pair of black, skinny jeans.

Her ensemble was almost a perfect color match to the uniforms Jonah and his teammates were wearing. Unfortunately, she was still in her kimono and all her clothes were laid out on her king-size bed. That's when I threatened to leave without her if she wasn't ready to go by five-thirty.

Since my mother needed another five minutes to fix her perfectly tousled hair, and then another five to find the right shade of lipstick, it was a wonder we had arrived at the gym with any time to spare at all.

"Come along, girls," Gram insisted, leading the way. "Let's find our seats before all the good ones are taken."

I aimed a smug smile at Marietta. "See? The best seats fill up fast. Now, move along."

My mother heaved a sigh. "There are plenty of seats. The stands aren't even half full."

"I know," I said, raising my voice over the sound of dozens of rubber soles squeaking against the surface of the polished hardwood as both teams ran drills under the baskets. "But you don't want to sit too far back or you won't be able to see Barry in action."

Especially since she refused to wear her glasses in public.

"I guess you have a point," my mother finally conceded, squinting at the two men in the Warriors hoodies and black slacks standing in front of a row of folding chairs. "Is that where he'll be most of the game?"

I didn't know where else a coach would sit. "Probably."

"Then we should sit somewhere up there," Marietta said, pointing toward the mid-court section of bleacher seats that we were approaching. "Oh, look. There's Veronica."

I scanned the small crowd of moms and dads occupying the first several rows and quickly spotted Veronica Lovely in the fourth-row aisle seat.

Yep, this was definitely where I wanted to sit, I thought, taking Gram's arm to help her up the steps while my mother gave her favorite would-be reality TV star a friendly wave.

"What a small world!" Marietta exclaimed in her typical, southern-fried fashion, pausing to chat with the smiling brunette sitting next to a cute nine- or ten-year-old girl. "You were the last person I thought I'd run into tonight."

"My son's on the team," Veronica said with a glance in Jonah's direction.

"Mah husband coaches the team!" My mother leaned in as if they were girlfriends exchanging secrets. "It's his first game, so we're here to cheer him on. And the team, of course."

Good one, Mom.

That provided all the cover I needed for being someplace I knew I didn't belong. But it didn't hurt to show some solidarity with our stated mission, so I added, "Go, Warriors!"

"Go, Warriors," Veronica responded, smiling at me like a greeter at a storefront. She had injected enough warmth to make me feel welcome, but not enough to encourage further conversation.

A split second later, her gaze shifted to someone else climbing the aisle steps and she motioned to her daughter. "Amelia, scoot over, honey."

That's when I saw the big guy in his mid-forties coming up behind us.

That's also when Gram tugged on my arm. "Grab your mother and let's get out of the aisle."

I tried the same arm-tug approach with Marietta, but she shook me off and smiled at the guy as if he were a fan approaching for a selfie.

"Hello there," she cooed.

Standing at least six foot four in all black and sporting a buzz cut that complemented his stony expression, he looked no-nonsense as opposed to the vivacious local celebrity blocking his path.

"Hi." He waited for a beat, annoyance tugging at his chiseled lips when she didn't move, and then gestured at the space Veronica had created for him. "That's my seat."

"Oh, *pardon*," Marietta tittered, sounding like an effusive French maître d' as she stepped out of his way.

He glowered at me and I took that as my cue to try the arm-tug again. "We should get Gram off her feet."

"Absolutely." Marietta gave Veronica a wave goodbye. "Enjoy the game."

"You, too," Veronica replied politely before shifting her attention to a whistle being blown on the court below us.

"Who the heck was that?" my mother asked me seconds later as we settled into our seats four rows back from Veronica and company.

I didn't think it was in my best interest to appear overly curious about the men in Veronica Lovely's life, especially the ones who looked like they could snap me like a twig. "Who do you mean?"

Marietta cocked her head. "Who do you think I mean? The hunky guy we just encountered."

Gram snickered on the other side of me. "He's rather attractive, if you like your men tall, dark, and full of muscles. Which I happen to think is mighty fine."

That sure wasn't the way I would have described my grandfather. "Gram, since when?"

"Oh, don't act so shocked. Just because I'm old doesn't mean I can't look." She shrugged. "I just do my looking from a safe distance."

I could relate, since that's exactly what I had come here to do.

"So who is he? Friend? Family?" Marietta sucked in a breath. "Or could he be a lover because that guy is dangerously handsome. Although it does seem a bit tacky to appear in public with your new man when your old one isn't in the ground yet."

True. But Veronica didn't strike me as someone who would do anything to tarnish her personal or professional reputation.

"He reminds me of someone I used to work with," my mother said, her voice trailing off for a second. "Oh, I know. Tony something. He had a recurring role in season two. Lovely man. Really built. If I'm remembering correctly, he'd been a competitive body builder and had a very good run in the 1980s playing hitmen and military bad-boy types."

I wouldn't be a bit surprised to learn that the hunk sitting next to Veronica was former military. He definitely looked the part. Dangerously handsome, too, in a solid and entirely male body. It didn't mean that he did bad things with that body.

But like Tony, if a bad-boy type was needed from central casting, this guy would sure fit the bill.

Gram turned to me. "Do you know who he is?"

"Nope," I said, snapping a quick photo of the guy with my phone.

But I intended to find out.

Chapter Seventeen

The next morning, while I was on my jog with Fozzie, I received a text from Steve.

Usually, his texts on the mornings we didn't wake up next to one another would contain some mention of a breakfast date. On the weekends, that breakfast would typically take place at my house since I was the one who had more than just a box of Cap'n Crunch in her pantry.

But instead of a breakfast date, he suggested dinner at his place, writing that he'd pick us up a couple of steaks after he caught up on some paperwork at the station.

"Works for me!" I texted back. *"See you around six."*

Which gave me most of the day to myself.

"Maybe I could do some catching up of my own," I said to Fozzie as we headed home.

Almost five hours later, I stepped through the door of Donatello's, the popular cut and curl owned by one of my besties, Donna Dearborn.

Just like Duke's Cafe, Donatello's was a hub for local

gossip. I also desperately needed a haircut, so it was fortunate timing when Donna had told me that she would be happy to squeeze me in at noon if I could bring her lunch, specifically a chicken and bacon ranch sub with extra cheese, potato chips, a carton of chocolate milk, and a big dill pickle from the Red Apple Market deli.

Yep, my buddy Donna was three months pregnant, not that anyone could tell by looking at the tiny baby bump hidden under her black stylist apron. But her cravings for all things salty were a dead giveaway.

She pounced on the bag of chips I was carrying before the door swung shut behind me. "You're a lifesaver," she said, tearing open the bag.

While Donna dropped into one of the two swivel salon chairs and crunched on a handful of chips, I laid out the rest of her lunch order on the countertop in front of her.

"I'm hardly a lifesaver," I said to her reflection in the mirror. "A week's worth of sodium is in that bag."

Smiling contentedly, she reached for another chip. "Bless your sodium-supplying heart."

"I don't see how you can eat like this and still be a size four."

"In my loosest sundress, maybe." Donna tugged on the elastic waistband of her blue jeans. "I've already graduated into preggo pants. Thankfully, Roxie saved all of hers, so I don't have to run out and do a bunch of shopping. Another lifesaver."

I forced a smile while feeling a slight pang of envy that Donna had inherited Rox's maternity clothes instead of me.

"These are a little big," she added between mouthfuls of potato chips. "But Ian's told me that big babies run in his family, so I fully expect to stretch this elastic to its limits."

"It's good to have a goal, but you don't have to try to achieve it in one day." I snatched the bag from her lap. "And I bought these to share, so stop being a chip hog."

Donna licked the salt from her fingertips and moaned in ecstasy. "I swear those things are addictive. They're all I've wanted to eat the last few days. Well, that and bacon."

After I shook out a small mountain of chips onto a napkin, I handed her back the bag. "Who am I to keep you from the ones you love."

Clutching the bag to her increasingly perky bosom, she grinned. "My feeling exactly."

"Speaking of loved ones," I said, taking advantage of the moment. "Maybe you can help identify someone I'm curious about."

Donna's sapphire eyes sparkled with interest. "As in someone involved in a case you're working on?"

"Nope. Just a friend of a friend I met the other night." Kind of.

I showed her my cell phone pic. "This guy."

Crunching another chip while she studied the image I had snapped at the game, Donna nodded approvingly. "Well, he's quite the studly-looking friend." She plucked the phone from my hand and enlarged the photo. "Is that bulge a gun under his jacket or does he have that much muscle?" she asked, pointing at his right side.

I took back my phone and studied the slight bulge I hadn't noticed before. "He had plenty of muscle, but it's probably just the way his jacket hangs on him."

Or a holstered pistol accounted for the bulge.

"And who is he exactly?" Donna asked.

Dang. I was hoping she could tell me that. "I have no idea."

"I thought you said you met him."

"We didn't exchange any personal details," I said, dropping my phone into my tote.

When I turned my attention back to Donna I noticed that she had set aside the bag of chips as if she'd suddenly lost her appetite. "What's the matter?"

"You tell me."

I didn't like her tone. "You're gonna have to give me a clue here."

"The stud that you're trying to get the deets on."

"What about him?"

Donna leaned forward in her chair. "Why are you so interested in him? Is he a suspect in some investigation that I haven't heard about?"

"No, no." This was a direction I didn't want to go.

"Like I said, he's a friend of a friend and I was just—" Hesitant to say more since she was almost as big of a gossip as Lucille.

"Just what?"

"Like I said, I was just curious about him."

Donna clucked her tongue. "I'm not buying this as idle curiosity. If he's not a suspect, are you trying to hook up with him or something?"

What? "No! Why would you even think that?"

"Because it feels like you've been dragging your feet about getting married, and now you're trying to find out the name of a hunky guy you encountered somewhere. I assume Steve wasn't with you at the time?"

I had to give Donna something or this conversation was going to spin out of control. "I happened to be with my mother and grandmother when we met up with this guy, and if you must know, it was my granny who couldn't take her eyes off him."

Donna scoffed. "Please don't try to convince me that you're worried about your grandma riding off into the sunset on the back of this guy's motorcycle."

"Hardly." I grabbed the white deli sack containing my sandwich and swiveled in the other chair to face her. "And I don't know if he even has a motorcycle." Although he'd probably score some points with Gram if he did. "I just thought he might be someone you knew, a client maybe."

"Nope. Never saw him before."

Then that was that, I thought, unwrapping my sandwich while Donna rattled the chip bag.

"If you're so interested, how come you haven't asked your friend who he is?" she asked.

"Uh..." I looked down at the sandwich on my lap as if a reasonable answer to that very reasonable question had been tucked under the lettuce leaf like a dab of secret sauce. "It's a little complicated to explain."

Donna sucked in a breath. "It's because this *is* connected to a case you're working on, isn't it?"

Crap. "Not officially, so I'd appreciate—"

"Okay, now we're getting somewhere!" She crunched on another chip. "So, who is he and what did he do?"

"Nothing." That I knew of. "He's just a guy who happened to show up somewhere."

"At a place you were staking out?"

Sort of.

"With my grandmother?" I rolled my eyes for dramatic effect.

"Fine. It wasn't a stake-out. It was just some sort of chance encounter and his presence piqued your interest. Is that what you want me to believe?"

"Yep." It was also what I needed her to believe.

"Okay. But if I happen to see the guy, like if he comes in for a trim, should I worry? Because if he's a criminal and he's wanted for armed robbery or something—"

"You don't need to worry about anything like that."

"Then what about you?" she asked, her gaze steady and penetrating. "Should I worry about you?"

I laughed her off. "He doesn't pose any danger to me." He only looked like he could.

Donna's expression softened. "I wasn't referring to your mystery man. I've been concerned about you ever since..."

I didn't want to hear what was coming.

I didn't want to think about it.

And while I appreciated her concern. And my mother's, and my grandmother's, and Rox's, it didn't make me any more eager to set a date than I was when I hung up on my wedding planner two months ago. So I stared at a scuff mark on one of Donna's black clogs and steeled myself for the heart-to-heart I wasn't prepared to have.

That's when the door swung open and Rox stepped in, pushing her thirteen-month-old in his travel stroller.

"Well, fancy meeting you here," she said to me.

Yeah, some fancy coincidence that she would show up at this precise moment. Almost as if it had been planned.

"Hi," I said before aiming a glare at Donna, which she deftly avoided by spinning to greet Rox.

"You have excellent timing." Donna held up the bag of chips. "Char brought lunch and there's plenty to share."

"And here I'd thought all I was gonna get was a haircut," Rox said, rolling a sleeping Alex toward me.

Since she also seemed to be avoiding eye contact, I smelled a rat. "Uh-huh. When's your appointment?"

Rox dragged one of the black fake leather chairs over from the waiting area. "Twelve-thirty." She flashed an innocent smile. "Donna's squeezing me in right after you."

Only I was the one feeling squeezed.

"Right after me?" I glanced at the clock centered between the two mirrors. "It's sixteen after now, and she hasn't even started on me, so do you want to try again?"

Rox blew out a sigh. "Nope. You'd know I'm lying, so I give up. I just wanted to see you."

"Which she had mentioned to me the last time we talked," Donna added. "So I invited her to join us for lunch. I knew you wouldn't mind."

The only thing I minded about this lunch gathering was that it suddenly felt like an ambush.

"Since we chatted for a few minutes when I stopped by for lunch Wednesday," I said to Rox. "Anything in particular on your mind?"

She and Donna exchanged nervous glances.

Good grief.

Using a spare napkin, I handed half of my sandwich to Rox. "If you're not going to say anything, I'm going to eat before this gets any colder than it already is."

"Fine. I'll just say it," she said just as I was about to take a bite. "We're a little worried about you."

I dropped my sandwich back to my lap. "If this is about the wedding, there's nothing to worry about." And nothing to add to what I had already told her.

"Easy for you to say," Donna stated around a mouthful of chips. "If you don't get married pretty soon, I won't have a prayer of fitting into my bridesmaid dress."

The burgundy lace sheath she had helped me pick out was so curve-hugging, she already didn't have that prayer. "Not to worry, we'll find you another dress. And I'll buy."

Donna waved me off. "Oh, honey, you don't have to do that."

Yes, I did. She had already paid for one bridesmaid dress. I couldn't ask her to pay for another. "Hey, I'm the one who got you into this situation."

She snickered. "Well, Ian helped."

"He definitely did his part," I cheerfully conceded. "But he didn't change the date of the wedding on you."

"Okay, fine. When do you want to go shopping?" Donna asked.

"I don't know." This wasn't something I wanted to think about right now. "Sometime after the holidays."

Donna exchanged the bag of potato chips for the day planner on the counter and grabbed a pen. "We'd better pick a date, or between your schedule and mine it'll never happen."

I stifled a groan.

She flipped a few pages. "How about the second Saturday in January? I don't have anyone scheduled after noon."

"I don't know." The phrase I kept repeating sounded emptier each time I said it. I also had the distinct impression that Donna wasn't listening to me when she pointed her pen at Rox.

"Want to come with?" Donna asked her. "We could make it a girls' afternoon out."

Rox brightened. "Sure! I'll see if my mom can babysit that day."

"Wait a minute," I said, loud enough to startle Alex. "I didn't say yes to this. I said sometime after the holidays, as in there's a lot going on right now, so let's decide on this later."

Rox set her half sandwich on the counter, picked up her crying baby, and then turned to Donna. "See how she is?"

Donna nodded. "Just like you said."

Excuse me? "What's that supposed to mean?"

With Alex burying his head in her shoulder, Rox

stepped in front of me. "For weeks now, everything's been 'later' with you."

"Especially when it comes to your wedding," Donna piled on.

"That's not true." Okay, maybe it was, but I didn't need my best friends pointing this out to me.

"I've hardly seen you since you called off your wedding," Donna said with a pretty pout. "And when I do, you barely want to talk. In fact, I think the only reason you called me this morning was because you wanted to show me that picture."

I could feel my cheeks flush as if Donna had set a match to the guilt I felt for having avoided her.

Rox's eyes narrowed. "What picture?"

"He's someone Char is 'unofficially' investigating." Donna waggled her pen at me. "Show her. Maybe she's seen him at Eddie's."

Fine. Rox would have been the next person on my list to ask if she recognized the guy, so this saved me a trip.

"Calling what I'm doing 'investigating' is overstating it." I reached down for my phone, opened my photos, and showed her the image of Mr. Dark and Dangerously Handsome. "This is just someone I ran into a couple of days ago and I was wondering who he was."

Rox squinted at the screen and shook her head. "He doesn't look familiar. Where'd you run into him?"

Nowhere I wanted to discuss. "I was out with my family and he happened to sit with someone we knew."

"I feel like I'm missing something," Rox said. "Why all the interest in this guy?"

I slapped a smile on my face. "Just curious if he was someone local."

"Just curious, huh? That's what you say every time you run across someone associated with Kevin Lovely."

Oops. I had forgotten I'd said pretty much the same thing after I found that picture of Kevin at Zack Wooten's birthday party.

Rox shifted Alex in her arms. "And I suppose this is the same picture you showed Sofia the other day."

"Nope." Trying to play it cool while Rox got too close for comfort, I dropped my phone back into my tote. "It's something completely different." Which happened to be conveniently true.

Rox smirked. "Sure."

"I swear," I said, making the three-finger salute like when we were Girl Scouts. "It's not the same picture."

She gave me a hard stare. "Okay, but I bet he has some connection to Kevin."

I eyed the wall clock. "Oh, look at the time. It's almost twelve-thirty and I have to be somewhere by one."

Where, I didn't know, but as long as it wasn't here I was good with that.

Donna pushed out of her chair. "But what about your haircut?"

"I can wait another week or two. Rox can have my appointment."

"That's not necessary," Rox protested.

Oh, yes it was, especially if I wanted to nip any discussion of Kevin Lovely in the bud.

"It's fine, really." I wrapped up the rest of my lunch

and bounded to my feet to hug them goodbye. "I'll see you soon."

"When?" Donna demanded. "'Cause, honey, you really do need those bangs trimmed."

The ones I had been pushing out of my eyes for the last month? Yes, I did, dang it. "This time next Saturday? I could even bring lunch again."

She reached for her day planner. "Maybe you'd even stay long enough to eat it."

"That'll be the plan." I kissed the top of Alex's head on my way to the door. "See you soon!"

Once I reached my car I realized Rox had followed me outside.

"We worry about you, you know," she said when I turned to face her.

"There's nothing to worry about."

"Just because you keep saying that doesn't mean I have to believe it."

"Well, it's true."

Rox inched closer while Alex waved his arms in the direction of a crow squawking in a nearby tree. "What's also true is that you seem more focused on what was going on in Kevin Lovely's love life than your own."

"No, I'm not." Although I could see how it looked that way. I was just helping out a friend. Not that Heather still qualified in that regard. "I'm just—"

"Asking questions. I know. It's what you do. Just remember that the answers you get won't do a darn thing to change the fact that he died in a fluky accident."

"Absolutely," I said to reassure my best friend.

But I wasn't so sure about that fluky accident part.

Chapter Eighteen

"I know," I said to Fozzie, who was giving me some serious side-eye from the passenger seat of my Subaru as I rifled through my tote bag for one of the sample tubes of lipstick my mother had given me. "I shouldn't care what Heather thinks."

But I did.

I'd always cared about what my childhood friend thought.

That's why, after I left Donna's shop, I had driven home to change into the designer jeans that made my legs look longer and the plum wrap sweater I had treated myself to while doing some early Christmas shopping in Seattle.

I had brushed my teeth to get the taste of bacon ranch out of my mouth and then spent the next half hour flat-ironing my hair and touching up my makeup.

I rarely made this much effort for a date with Steve. The reason being that he preferred to see me naked.

But this was Heather Beckett I had dressed for. The gorgeous former prom queen, who typically looked as if she had stepped out of a fashion magazine.

She was the perfect model for the clothes of the high-end Port Townsend boutique, where she was sure to be working on this busy holiday season shopping day.

So I'd be meeting her on her turf instead of a neutral site like the dog park. And for that I wanted to look good, preferably with a more neutral shade of lipstick because the Passionate Plum I'd applied to go with my sweater screamed that I was trying too hard.

I was. I didn't need Fozzie's side-eye to tell me as much.

"Besides, you're supposed to be my comfort animal on this little adventure," I reminded him. "You should at least give me a tail wag of support."

He huffed as if this wasn't his idea of a fun adventure.

I couldn't blame him. There wasn't a green space or another dog anywhere close to where I had parked.

"We'll hit the dog park before we go home," I promised him as my fingertips landed on a tube of Bronze Goddess from the Glorious Organics line of cosmetics Marietta repped. "Perfect."

I flipped down my visor, blended in the glossy bronze, and then flashed a toothy grin at my reflection to check for lipstick smears. "Not exactly perfect." But this suited me better and would have to do.

I would go to the boutique, tell Heather that I was shopping for a Christmas present for my mother, which happened to be true. Then I'd casually mention that I saw Kevin's widow with someone.

No doubt, Heather would find this suspicious, since

she remained adamant that Veronica was to blame for her husband's death. Which would then afford me a choice opportunity to see if Heather could identify him.

After striking out with Donna and Rox, I had no one else I trusted to ask short of going to Veronica herself, which wasn't an option since I barely knew the woman. Nor did I want her to think I was intruding into her personal life.

Which I totally was. But I didn't want to be obvious about it.

With my plan in place, I cracked open the windows in my car for Fozzie, then set out for Mirabella's, the over-priced women's clothing store situated on Water Street between a trendy cafe and a funky gift shop that featured local artisans.

My mother liked to brag about supporting her fellow local artists, so I made a mental note to hit the gift shop to buy her something one of a kind before I left town.

Inhaling the alluring aroma of the coffee they roasted at Fresh Harvest Eatery, I paused to check my reflection in their window. The gray clouds hovering over town had cooperated and not rained on me, but the wind gusting from the north had done a number on my hair.

I quickly smoothed it into place, took a deep breath, and then with my heart pounding as if I were about to enter enemy territory, I opened the door to Mirabella's.

The little bell mounted over the doorway announced my presence while the fresh air that came in with me stirred the cinnamon scent of the basket of pine cones in the display window.

Heather, standing behind a customer service counter as she assisted a grandmotherly type, glanced over with a polite smile hanging from her lips. "Be right with you."

Then her expression froze as she met my gaze.

I know. Until a couple of hours ago, I hadn't expected to see you today either.

I gave her a little wave. "No rush, I'm just going to browse."

Before a minute passed, a pretty twenty-something with soft brown curls that fell past her shoulders approached me while I fingered the fabric of a cranberry cable knit sweater.

"It's cotton blended with locally sourced alpaca wool and hand-knit," she told me reverentially.

Of course it was. As reflected by the price tag.

"Perfect for the holidays," she continued. "And the color would be great on you."

"I'm actually looking for a gift," I said loud enough to be heard by the salesperson with the blond-streaked chignon heading in our direction.

"Hi, Charmaine. Doing some Christmas shopping?" Heather asked.

And then some.

I nodded. "My mom's hard to shop for, but maybe you can help me."

With that the other girl backed off, probably assuming that her coworker and I were old friends, or at least close acquaintances.

Both felt oddly true, especially lately.

"Marietta's taste tends to run expensive and showy,

so I thought..." I'd come to your shop in search of something gaudy and overpriced? Nope. I didn't want to suggest that Heather's presence wasn't the only reason I didn't shop here. "I thought I might find..." Something eclectic but within my budget? That would make me sound like a former TV star's poor and snobby relation. I didn't want to suggest that either.

"You thought right by coming here." Heather brightened, stepping closer when her coworker moved to the far wall to assist another customer. "We specialize in expensive and showy, although we prefer to think of it as quality chic."

"That's what I meant to say," I quipped.

"I take it this sweater isn't quite what you're looking for."

"It's a bit more than what I'd planned to spend."

She nodded as if she'd taken a peek at my last paycheck. "We're having a holiday sale. Everything in this section is ten percent off, and all the items in the back of the store are marked down twenty-five percent."

I immediately started moving in the direction of the greater savings. "Maybe I should check that out."

Five minutes of combing through three racks of winter-weather clothes later, I found a black tunic-length sweater with decorative turquoise, teal, and rose feather-like swirls. "What do you think?" I asked Heather, when she lingered at a nearby table to straighten a stack of polos.

"That's one of my favorite pieces in the store." Heather plucked a scoop neck shell in the same shade of rose from the rack behind her. "It's especially 'showy' with this top." Her full lips curled like they used to when we were kids sharing a private joke. "Assuming that's the look you're going for."

She already knew that it was.

I tried the sweater on for size. Too small for me would be perfect for my more petite mother.

"It suits you," Heather said, following me to the full-length mirror on the back wall. "And it's quite striking with your coloring."

While I couldn't detect any guile in her words, it didn't seem natural for Heather to say anything complimentary toward me.

I shrugged off the sweater. "It's a little tight."

Since it was two sizes smaller than the wrap sweater I was wearing, more than a little.

I waited for her placid expression to falter, for some little bubble of condescension to rise to the surface. But that didn't happen.

Instead, Heather pointed to the indigo and lavender knit top she wore over navy slacks. "If I tried that on over this, it would be tight on me too."

I seriously doubted that, but I had long ago been trained by my grandmother to not call out the little lies intended to make me feel better. "That's okay. It should fit my mother just fine."

"If it doesn't, she can exchange it for something else she'd like."

Which would require a trip back here, with my mother wanting to make a girls' day out of the occasion.

That made me think of the shopping excursion Donna had tried to arrange, and a sigh escaped my lips.

"I'm sure she'll like it if that's a concern," Heather said.

"I'm sure she will." Well, as sure as I could be of anything Marietta hadn't picked out herself. "I was just thinking about some other shopping I needed to do."

"More Christmas shopping?"

She had just given me an easy out. "Yep."

Heather hesitated for a beat. "Here in Port Townsend?"

I wasn't sure why she would want to know that, but it seemed like an innocuous-enough question. "I thought I'd hit the gift shop next door before I headed home. They always have fun things."

Heather cracked a fake smile as if she had exhausted her supply of polite chitchat held in reserve for former friends.

I figured that was my cue to hand her the sweater and coordinating shell so that she could ring up my purchase.

When I got to the customer service counter in the center of the store, I pulled out my cell phone as well as my wallet. Fortunately, there would be no one within earshot to hear me ask the "other woman" if she recognized the man sitting next to Veronica Lovely.

After Heather processed my credit card, she wrapped the sweater and top in white tissue paper and placed it in a gift box. "Thanks for coming in," she said like a customer service automaton, bagging the box and passing it over the counter to me.

Just when I raised my phone to show her that photo, Heather lowered her voice. "Can you wait for me next door? I need to speak with you."

I didn't need to guess what about.

"Sure." The other salesperson was heading in our direction, so a more private location could benefit both of us.

But after a few minutes of browsing the aisles of the crowded gift shop, I joined Heather when I saw her standing by the door. "There's no place to talk in here. Where—"

"Come with me," she said, holding the door open.

I followed her down a narrow alley that separated Fresh Harvest from one of Gram's favorite antique stores. This sheltered us from the swirling wind, but there was a powerful stench rising from the rusting dumpster in the back, so I was relieved when Heather stopped under a vent infusing our air space with the aroma of the roast of the day.

She turned to me. "Did you give that envelope to Steve like I asked you to?"

Evidently, he hadn't followed up with her—something that didn't bother me in the slightest. "Yes."

"Did he say anything to you about it?"

Only that it hadn't contained a love letter, which she would find even less amusing than I did. "He didn't say a thing."

"I thought he might at least..." Heather hugged her arms to her chest as if she needed the emotional support. "I guess it doesn't matter what I thought."

"He doesn't talk to me about anything he's working on." Much to my frustration. "You might want to follow up with him if there's something specific you wanted to ask him."

She choked out a humorless chuckle. "Yeah. My prior efforts to 'follow up' have been so successful."

"If you don't mind me asking, what was in the envelope?"

"Everything I knew about what happened the day Kevin died."

I had assumed that Steve already had this information. He had certainly acted as if there hadn't been anything illuminating in that envelope. "Like what?"

"The exact time he called to tell me he was leaving early. Four twenty-two," Heather stated as if by rote. "The call lasted three minutes. Before Kevin disconnected, he specifically said he was on his way. His exact words were, 'See you in ten.' So, I know for a fact that he left his house around four twenty-five."

And I knew for a fact that she called Steve close to an hour later. All this proved nothing. "That was Kevin's intention, anyway. Maybe something happened to delay him, maybe something with one of the kids, and he didn't leave until—"

"His engine was running. I could hear his radio!"

"But you don't know the exact time that he went off the road."

That earned me a few choice curse words, and Heather started to walk away.

"I'm sorry," I said, catching up with her. "It's just that there are other witness statements that conflict—"

"Oh, I know, and I'm sure that Veronica was real convincing when she finally called 911. Acting like it was some sort of accident that had *just* happened."

"You don't know when—"

"I know when Kevin stopped answering his phone!" Heather whirled around to face me, her volume turning heads of the passersby streetside. "Five o'clock exactly! Know how I know that? Because that's when I called to ask if he had stopped to get a pizza or something. But it went to voice mail, just like the other two times I called. No call backs, no texts, which wasn't like him at all. He always called me back."

Kevin Lovely, the courteous serial cheater.

"That's when I knew something was very wrong." Heather's voice broke, her blue eyes gleaming with tears.

"I have my call log that shows all the times, how long we spoke—everything. It's proof that there's at least a full hour between when Kevin said he was leaving and that 911 call. That's a lot of time that's unaccounted for. Not that Steve cares."

I didn't feel particularly honor-bound to defend my fiancé to his old girlfriend, but I had to say something. "He cares."

Okay, that sounded lame. I tried again. "We both care."

"Right." With a sniff Heather tossed her head back as if to shake off the tears. "I'm touched."

Checking the pink smartwatch at her wrist, she set

her feet in motion. "I need to get back to work."

Crap! Our caring moment might be over, but I still needed her help identifying the mystery man sitting next to Veronica.

"Heather, wait!" Fumbling for my phone, I trotted after her.

"There isn't anything else to say," she said dismissively. "In fact, I'm sorry I got you involved in this."

"Well, it's a little late for that." I wasn't sure that I wanted to be entirely honest with her, but I needed to give her a good reason to stick around for a few more minutes. "Because something doesn't feel right to me about Kevin's accident."

Heather stopped in her tracks. "Because it *wasn't* an accident."

I couldn't go that far, not when Steve and Ben had come to the opposite conclusion. "Maybe. I don't have a lot to go on. I just get the sense that there's more to this than anyone's been willing to talk about."

"That's what I've been saying!" Heather declared. "So, what are we going to do about it?"

We?

What was she suggesting? That we team up to peck all around Steve's investigation like a pair of free-range chickens? He would fricassee me first and ask questions later. Not this chick's idea of fun foreplay.

"People might be more willing to open up to me than you since...well, you know," I said, hoping that she'd fill in the blank.

Heather's glossy lips drew into a pensive smirk.

"Since I'm the evil homewrecker."

Not the exact description I would have used, but I wasn't about to argue the point. "Just let me see what I can find out."

"Fine," Heather bit out as if it were anything but. "You promise to keep me informed?"

"I promise. In fact, I already have something I wanted to share with you." I opened the camera app on my phone and showed her the last photo I took. "Do you recognize this guy?"

She shook her head. "He doesn't look familiar."

Dang it! She had been my best hope to ID him.

"Who is he?" she asked.

"I don't know yet. He was sitting next to Veronica when I took the picture."

Heather's eyes widened with interest. "Really."

"He's a big, strong-looking guy, maybe six-four or five. Did Kevin ever mention anyone like that?"

"No."

"Or maybe mention a man in Veronica's life?"

"She wasn't a subject that came up much. As you can imagine, he wasn't with me to talk about her. But if he'd known that she was seeing someone, I'm sure he would have said something."

But he didn't, and I was no closer to finding out the man in black's identity than I was last night.

Heather checked her watch again. "If there's nothing else, I really need to get back."

"Give me just a sec. I have one more picture that I wanted to show you," I said, finding the photo of Kevin and Scarlett at Zack Wooten's birthday party. Zooming in to only show Zack's face, I sidled up next to Heather. "Do you know this guy?"

"Yeah, he's Zack somebody. Kevin told me that he was someone he knew through work."

Through work as in through Scarlett? "That's it? He didn't elaborate?"

"No. Now if you'll excuse me, I've got to go," Heather said, marching toward the alley entrance.

"Hold up." I ran to catch up with her, my shopping bag bouncing against my thigh and slowing me down. "Did you get the impression that they were friends?"

"I only saw the guy once and it was from a distance when we stopped at a convenience store. But given Kevin's mood when he got back in the car, no. This wasn't someone he was happy to spend time with."

"When did this happen?"

"I know it was a Saturday night. Probably the week after Halloween."

"And you just happened to stop at this convenience store when Zack was there."

Heather frowned. "Sort of. On the way home from dinner, Kevin said that he needed to get something."

"He was driving?"

She nodded.

"And where's this store exactly?"

"It's on the south end of Sims Way. Just past the car wash."

The car wash didn't help narrow it down for me. I had never once stopped in Port Townsend to wash my car.

Now, if she had mentioned an ice cream shop or pizza place on that block, I would have been able to avoid the blank look I gave her.

Heather huffed an impatient breath. "You'll drive right by it on your way out of town. You can't miss it. It's the car wash with the big bubbles on the sign."

I took her word for it. "Okay, so while you two were headed back to Port Merritt, Kevin said that he needed something from the convenience store. There'd been no mention of Zack up to this point, right?"

She nodded.

"And prior to Kevin saying that he needed to make a stop, everything had seemed pretty normal?" "Normal" being a relative term for a man who wouldn't want any of his wife's friends to see him out with another woman.

"Not really. He kept checking the time on his phone. I'd assumed it was because he needed to be home before the kids went to bed. But later I realized it was to meet up with this Zack guy."

That made my heart skip a beat. "You're sure?"

"Kevin never said so outright, but it seemed obvious once we got there."

And it seemed obvious to me that I'd better start taking notes, so I dropped my shopping bag to the rutted pavement and fished out a pad and pen from my tote. "Okay, I know you need to get back to work, but I want you to tell me everything you remember after Kevin said he needed to make a stop."

She gave me a pained look. "I already told you most of this."

Yes, but I wasn't taking notes at the time. "Start at the beginning this time. Please," I added with a sweet as sugar smile.

Heather heaved a sigh. "Fine. We pull in a few minutes before nine and I notice a guy sitting in an old Mustang parked around the side. I assumed that he works there and that he's waiting for the top of the hour when his shift starts or something. But as soon as Kevin steps out of the store, I see the guy get out of his car and walk up to him."

"Did Kevin seem surprised to see him?" I asked, scribbling as quickly as I could.

"It didn't look that way to me."

"Okay, then what?"

"They started talking. Talked for at least two or three minutes."

"Could you hear what they were saying?"

Heather shook her head. "They kept their voices pretty low. They even went over close to where Zack had parked, like they wanted privacy."

"Did you ask Kevin what that was about after he got back in the car?" Because I sure would have if I'd been along for this kind of obvious meet-up.

"Yeah, I asked who that was, but he didn't say much. It was like he needed to cool down first. He smoked a cigarette—something I'd never seen him do before—and then finally he told me that the guy's name was Zack and that he met him through a mutual work acquaintance."

I assumed this was before Kevin knocked up this acquaintance.

I looked up from my notepad when Heather stopped talking. "That's it?"

"Yeah, he wouldn't talk about whatever it was that they exchanged."

"What do you mean, 'exchanged'?"

"Handed to one another," Heather deadpanned, her tone suggesting that I should work on expanding my vocabulary.

Cute. "I meant what was it that they exchanged?"

"All I saw was that something changed hands."

"Like in a drug buy," I said, thinking aloud about what would typically change hands after dark in a parking lot.

"I don't know. Like I told you, I'd never even seen Kevin smoke a cigarette before. When I asked about it, he said it was nothing."

It didn't sound like nothing to me. "Anything else?"

"No. Kevin might have seemed a little preoccupied for most of the drive home, but I didn't make that much out of it. I figured that if it was something he wanted me to know, he would've told me."

Really? I found it hard to believe that she wouldn't have asked more questions, but I hadn't gotten the sense that she'd said one word that wasn't true. "So, you two never talked about this again?"

Heather shook her head.

"Did Zack's name come up any other time?" I asked.

"Not once. And that's all I know."

Then that was that. "Okay, I'll see what else I can find out about the guy."

I snapped my notepad shut, dropped it back into my

tote, and collected my bag. When I straightened, I had expected to see her irritatingly shapely butt in motion. Instead, Heather was staring at me with watery eyes.

Sheesh, was she going to cry again?

Her mouth opened and closed.

"Did you think of something else?" Because she obviously had something she wanted to say.

"No. I just…" Heather enveloped me in her arms and squeezed. "Thank you. You're the only one who's been willing to listen to me."

With my tote in one hand and my shopping bag in the other, I couldn't hug her back. Plus, I didn't want to. We weren't friends. We had barely been on speaking terms for decades prior to last weekend, and a couple of meet-ups to talk about her dead lover didn't miraculously change that.

As if sensing my spine stiffening under her touch, she immediately released me. "Too much?"

Heck, yes! "Don't be silly."

"For a human lie detector, you're a horrible liar."

"I…" I didn't know what to say.

"All I was trying to do was to say thank you. You know, like a normal person." Heather took a step toward Mirabella's and then glanced back at me. "So try not to make things overly weird between us."

Oh, it was way too late for that.

Chapter Nineteen

Almost two hours later, I let myself into Steve's house and found him marinating a couple of thick sirloin steaks in the kitchen.

His gaze roamed the length of me as I approached. "You look nice."

I'd fixed my hair and makeup after I got back from a breezy walk through the dog park with Fozzie and had thought the same thing when I left my house, so it felt good to see the appreciation in his eyes for my efforts.

Even though Steve wasn't the one I had dressed to impress today.

"I like this." He ran his fingers over the opening of my sweater and then grinned rakishly at the bit of cleavage he had revealed. "I like what's inside of it even more."

Wrapping my arms around his waist, I breathed in his clean scent while lifting my chin to give him a quick kiss. "I'm assuming you mean my sparkling personality."

"That too."

"Uh-huh." Pushing him away, I scanned his white tile countertop for salad fixings, some veggies in need of chopping—something to accompany the meatfest.

"What can I do?" I started to open the refrigerator door to see if I could answer my own question, but Steve quickly blocked my path.

"Absolutely nothing, because I'm the cook tonight." Taking me by the shoulders, he directed me to the closest of the four chairs surrounding his kitchen table. "So, you get to sit here and keep me company."

"I take it that means that we're having steak, potatoes, and nothing much that's green," I said, admiring the way his blue jeans rode on his narrow hips.

"Needless filler. But since you insist on having a vegetable..." Steve retrieved a carton of button mushrooms from his refrigerator and cradled it like an offering to the god of steak sides. "I'll be sauteing these babies."

The last time he sauteed mushrooms, they were buttery restaurant quality, so I knew Steve had tonight's meal well in hand and settled back in my chair. "Yum."

I watched him open the bottle of pinot noir next to the stove where his mother used to grill the best cheese sandwiches and smiled at the memory. "Your mom would love seeing you getting all domestic in her kitchen."

Steve looked over as he reached for a wineglass. "She'll get that opportunity soon enough."

Huh? "What do you mean?"

"Since I have to work and won't be going to Santa Fe for Christmas, she and Gavin are coming here for a few days the week after next. Sort of an early Christmas."

"When did this get decided?" Because Steve hadn't

mentioned anything about his mother and stepfather coming to town.

"My mom called with the news about an hour before you got here." He handed me the wineglass. "Surprise!"

"Great." I took a sip of wine and wished that I could feel happy about this news. But all I could think about was how my mother would want to host us all for another elaborate dinner at her house, and I didn't want to poison Gavin and make a really bad first impression.

Steve nodded. "I know what you're thinking."

"I seriously doubt that."

"This has nothing to do with our wedding."

Given how his mother had twice mentioned that she needed the date so they could make their travel arrangements, I had my doubts about that too.

"Gavin has a brother who lives near Salem, and Mom's been a little homesick, so they'll be making the rounds visiting family and friends." Steve's gaze softened. "Of course, the most important family member they want to spend time with is you."

"Aww." I had always loved Steve's mother, and Gavin, the Santa Fe podiatrist she married four years ago, sounded like a great guy.

"It will be nice to finally meet Gavin in person." We had met last year, when Steve and I called via video chat to wish him a happy birthday.

"He's looking forward to that, too." Steve smirked. "Fair warning, he's eager to meet your mother since he missed out on doing that in Hawaii."

I cringed at the memory of telling Debbie and Gavin

that we were postponing the wedding. They were supportive and said all the right things, but I also felt their frustration with me.

And I didn't blame them one bit.

"That's easy enough to arrange," I said, trying to push aside the memory of that phone call. "Maybe we could all go out to dinner. Or you and I could host the parents here, or at my place, or—"

He silenced me with a kiss. "As long as that last option isn't eating at your mother's house, I'm good with whatever you want to do."

I lifted my glass. "I'll drink to that."

"Me too," Steve said, stealing my glass to take a long swallow. Then he made a face. "Not my favorite red, but it should be okay for sautéing as long as I add plenty of butter."

"The wine's fine." He was just more of a beer drinker. "But you're right about the butter. Never skimp on the butter."

"That's what a pastry chef once told me." He winked at me. "Maybe more than once to make sure I got the message."

"She sounds pushy."

"Nah. She's pretty great."

"If your pastry chef buddy is so great, she should have made us something for dessert."

"No need. Because while I was at the store I got something for us." He opened the refrigerator and gestured toward the small plastic container on the second shelf as if it were a prize in a game show. "A lava cake."

"Yum!" I had a weakness for ooey, gooey molten lava cake.

Heck, I had a weakness for anything that combined butter, flour, and chocolate, which he knew all too well.

"I got the last one. Found it in their individual serving section." Steve shut the refrigerator, signaling that show and tell was over.

"Individual, as in single serving."

"Right."

"Then what are *you* going to have for dessert?"

He aimed a wicked grin at me. "I have something else in mind."

"Something yummy?" I asked, closing the distance between us.

"I like to think so, but maybe you should be the judge." Lowering his head, Steve kissed me long and deliciously slowly.

Several skips of my heartbeat later, he held me at arm's length. "So, what do you think?"

What did I think? As if I were capable of rational thought while my insides melted like hot lava cake?

"Definitely yummy," I said, noticing the bulge straining the zipper of his jeans. "Perhaps while those steaks marinate, we could treat ourselves to dessert."

Because when the occasion called for it, I was a dessert-first kind of girl.

Chapter Twenty

"Debbie and Gavin Fordham are coming to town," I told Gram on the way home from church the next morning.

She gave me a confused look from the passenger seat. "Who?"

"Steve's mom and her husband."

"Oh, *that* Debbie. I've known her as Debbie Sixkiller for so long that it sounds funny to hear her new name."

I imagined that Steve felt the same way, although I knew he was happy that his mother had found such a good guy in Gavin, a widower with twin girls in their early thirties.

"When are they arriving?" Gram asked, interrupting my thoughts as we rounded the corner and headed for her house.

"The week before Christmas. Steve said they'd be here for a few days then they'll be off to Salem to visit family."

Gram reached into her purse, her keys jingling into her palm. "Sounds like it will be an early Christmas celebration here then."

"With all of us getting together for dinner one night. I

don't know any more than that right now," I said, pulling into her driveway. "But when I talk to Mom I'll ask which nights she and Barry are free that week, and we'll go from there."

"And where would this get-together be?"

"That's to be determined. Steve and I batted around some ideas, but that's as far as we got last night."

Gram wrapped her hand around my wrist the second we rolled to a stop. "You know your mother will insist on hosting as soon as you tell her that Debbie's coming to town."

"I know."

She tightened her grip. "That can't happen. We don't want a repeat of Thanksgiving."

"Trust me. I know that too. I'll make it very clear that this is an invitation to dinner with Steve's parents. And I'll say that it's at my house. That will make it even more obvious that all she and Barry need to do is show up."

Gram patted my hand as if I needed moral support. "Be strong."

"I know how to talk to her. It'll be fine."

"No, Mom, listen," I said almost two hours later, walking home from the dog park with Fozzie.

"Or maybe we could do a goose—a nice Christmas goose. I've never cooked a goose before. Not literally, anyway! But that could be fabulous."

I clenched my teeth with the certainty that my goose would be cooked if I didn't wrestle back control of this conversation. Pronto. "Actually—"

"Where does one buy goose? I think we'd want a fresh one."

"You don't—"

"Don't tell me. I know that might be difficult to find in town. Oh, I have it! Cornish game hens! I've seen those in the store."

"Mom!" I yelled over the rumble of a delivery truck blasting past me on 2nd Street.

"Where are you? It's very loud there. Are you able to hear me okay?"

"I can hear you just fine," I said, feeling like my cell phone was overheating, probably from all the steam that had been coming out of my ear. "But I don't think you're hearing me. Steve and I are inviting you and Barry to join us for dinner, as in all you have to do is show up."

"But my darling, your house is too small. Where's everyone going to sit?"

She had a point, dang it. I had a pedestal table that sat six, perfect for my cozy rental house. Not so perfect for a dinner party of seven.

"Did I say my house? I meant Steve's. It's not my house yet," I chuckled, trying to laugh my mistake away as if I'd made a Freudian slip. "He has that big dining room table and plenty of space for the seven of us." His selection of cookware was spartan at best, but I could bring over everything I needed to prepare the meal. It would be a lot like the last dinner party I worked for a caterer friend of mine.

I was a former pro who knew better than to leave anything to chance. Success depended upon preparation.

And now that I had a plan I could have confidence in, I just needed my mother to accept her role as guest. "When you were there for Gram's birthday dinner, you even remarked about how comfortable his sofa was, so it'll work out just fine there."

"Right," she muttered. "If that's what you would prefer."

The disapproval Marietta had injected into every syllable came through loud and clear. I didn't care. This wasn't her dinner party, and for the safety of all concerned as well as my sanity, it couldn't be.

"It will be perfectly nice. Maybe Cornish game hens could be on the menu like you were thinking." Which actually sounded festive as well as super-easy. "I have a great cranberry and apple stuffing recipe that I think you'd like. It looks very pretty on the plate too."

She didn't respond with anything beyond a disgruntled huff.

I pretended that I hadn't heard it. "Another good company dish would be au gratin potatoes. You know, the ones with the crusty cheese topping." Which my mother had raved about last Christmas. "And then for color and for those of us who want some lower-calorie options, we could have an assortment of herb-roasted carrots and brussels sprouts. How's that sound?"

"Fine," she stated flatly, sounding like she could do voiceover work as a sulky teenager.

"Okay, then. We've got our menu." Steve wouldn't be crazy about the brussels sprouts, but he could pick around them.

"If you wouldn't mind, would you select some wine to pair with our meal? You're so much better at that than I am." Because when perusing the wine aisle, I typically let the price be my guide.

"Of course," she said with an assurance that sounded so practiced I couldn't tell if my dollop of praise had managed to smooth any ruffled feathers. "Let me know if there's anything else I can do to help."

"Will do."

Several seconds of awkward silence ticked by, broken up only by the sound of my breathing as I tried to keep pace with Fozzie.

"Okay, then." If Marietta didn't have anything else to say, it was time to end this conversation, especially now that I was climbing the crest of the hill to my house. "I'll—"

"Charmaine?"

"Uh-huh."

"Your dinner sounds very nice."

I had a feeling that a *but* was coming. "Thanks. It'll be great way to kick off the holiday." Preferably with everyone on their best behavior and no emergency trips to the hospital.

"But…"

And here it came.

"Are you quite sure you wouldn't rather host Debbie and Gavin at my house?" she asked.

How many times did we need to go over this? "I'm—"

"Didn't you tell me that Steve barbecues everything

because he has hardly any cookware?"

Me and my big mouth. "He has a very nice grill and he enjoys using it."

"And I've seen that old stove of his. It hardly looks reliable."

"It works just fine." According to Steve. I thought it ran hot and had long ago decided it would be the first thing in his kitchen to go after we got married.

"Really, sweetheart. Wouldn't you rather prepare this meal at my house? We have every dish and gadget you could possibly need, every modern convenience, plus a Sub-Zero refrigerator with oodles of storage space."

"I..." *Shoot!* I couldn't think of one advantage Steve's house would have over my mother's.

"I assume while Debbie and Gavin are in town, they'll be staying with Steve?"

He had a guest room, so that had been my assumption. "Probably."

"So there's a likelihood they'd all be there while you're cooking, wanting to pitch in and help. As I recall, his kitchen isn't *that* big."

I hadn't thought that far ahead.

Walking past a fenced yard, I caught a whiff of chicken sizzling on a nearby grill.

Either that or my goose was indeed being cooked.

"I, on the other hand, would leave you alone. You'd have the entire kitchen to yourself," Marietta added, her voice rising and falling as if she were telling a bedtime story. "Why, you'd hardly even know I was in the house."

"Fine." So much for being the one who knew exactly

what to say to her. "We'll do this at your place."

"Goody!"

Yeah, goody.

"I'll have Steve confirm the date with Debbie and will get back to you," I said, following Fozzie's lead as he powered up the drive of my butter-yellow rental house.

Marietta was rambling on about restocking her liquor cabinet when Donna pulled up behind me in her Mini Cooper and rolled down the window.

"Hey, you!" she called out with a bright smile.

"What does Gavin drink, do you know?" my mother asked.

"I have no idea, and I've gotta go," I said, relieved for the happy excuse to disconnect and pocket my phone. At least I hoped it would be happy.

Since Donna hadn't gotten out of the car, I bent over at her window. "What's up?" Then I noticed she wasn't alone. Donna's eleven-year-old stepdaughter, Peyton, was crawling from the back seat to the front.

I waved at her. "Hi, Peyton."

"Hi, Miss Digby," she said, sitting tall on her heels with her big blue eyes focused on Fozzie.

The formality of being called "Miss Digby" always made me cringe. Peyton's father, Fozzie's veterinarian, had been a stickler about good manners when he introduced us last year in the dog park, which was something I could appreciate.

But that was then. "I think you should call me Char, don't you? Especially when it's just us girls."

Peyton turned to Donna, who nodded with an easy

grin. "What happens between us girls stays between us girls. Kind of like those milkshakes we had after lunch. Your dad doesn't need to find out about that."

Peyton giggled. "I like this girl stuff."

I suspected she liked having Donna as her stepmom even more.

With one of his favorite little humans mere feet away, Fozzie whimpered and strained at his leash.

"I bet I know something else you'd like," I said to Peyton. "Since I obviously didn't tire out my dog, do you want to play with him in the backyard?"

With a happy squeal, she scrambled out of the car and ran to Fozzie.

After handing Peyton the leash, I held Donna's door open for her. "I hope that's okay. You're not in a rush to get home, right?"

She gave her head a shake, her typically perky demeanor having shifted into an atypical neutral as she straightened. "I was hoping you'd have a few minutes to talk."

That wasn't what I had been hoping for since I wanted to dash up to Port Townsend this afternoon and see what else I could find out about Zack, but that could wait.

"What's wrong? Do you feel okay?" I asked after Peyton stepped through the fence gate with Fozzie and out of earshot.

"I'm fine, and nothing's wrong." Donna shot me a nervous glance as I reached into my pocket for my house key. "At least I hope not."

I stifled a groan. "This isn't about yesterday at the salon, is it?"

"Sort of."

Now what?

After opening the door, I headed for the kitchen. "Want some coffee?" Because I sure did, especially if Donna wanted to continue where she and Rox left off.

"Can't have the caffeine."

"Oh, yeah. I can make a pot of decaf."

"No thanks, but I'll take a glass of water."

Good. I hated decaf.

I filled a tumbler and set it on the kitchen table in front of Donna.

Taking a small sip, she grimaced as if her back hurt.

"Are you okay here? We could go into the living room where—"

"Stop worrying, I'm fine. The more important question is, are *we* okay?"

I dropped into the chair next to her. "Why wouldn't we be?"

Making a face as if I were being slow on the uptake, Donna cocked her head.

"Oh. You mean after yesterday's little ambush?"

"Please don't call it that."

"That's how it felt, so unless you have a better word for it—"

"I have several because it was an expression of love. We're your best friends and we're concerned about you. That's all."

"Well, you don't have to worry about me either. I'm

fine."

"That's what you keep saying."

"Because it's true."

Scowling, Donna folded her arms over her growing tummy. "Uh-huh."

"Really."

She stared at me in stony silence for several seconds. "Well, something is going on with you. I've hardly seen you for weeks!"

"I've just been busy. You know, with work and the holidays—"

"You seem to have plenty of time for Heather Beckett."

By Donna's tone it was obvious that someone had brought her some juicy gossip about seeing me with Heather.

Now it was my turn to stare in silence at Donna.

"You went to see her after walking out on me and Roxie," Donna continued as if I'd committed some sort of personal betrayal. "And don't even try to deny it. I have a witness."

"Then she must have seen me Christmas shopping in Port Townsend. That's where I happened to bump into Heather."

"In an alley? 'Cause that's where Crystal Zimmerman saw you two yelling at one another."

I remembered Crystal from high school as someone who liked to stick her turned-up nose where it didn't belong. Evidently, not much had changed.

Donna smirked. "She just *happened* to mention that

when she came in for a trim yesterday afternoon."

"Well, don't believe everything you hear."

"Honey, I know I can't tell when people are lying like you can, but Crystal wouldn't have any reason—"

"I know. But it wasn't the way she's making it sound."

"Then how was it?"

That wasn't a question that I could easily answer. "Heather's been upset about some stuff that I can't really get into, and Crystal must've walked by when things got a little heated."

Her smirk vanished. "This has to do with Kevin Lovely's death, doesn't it?"

There was no point in denying it, so I nodded.

Donna sharply inhaled. "This is the unofficial case you're working on! The one you wouldn't talk about yesterday."

"I'm not working on anything having to do with his death." Which was what I needed her to say in case this subject ever came up in front of Steve. "It was an accident, and all I'm trying to do is to tie up some loose ends."

"One of those loose ends being that hunky guy you were asking me about?"

"Yeah, but I wouldn't make too much of—"

"You know who you should ask to see if she recognizes him? Crystal."

I wasn't eager to invite Crystal Zimmerman to get more involved in my business than she already was. "I don't know—"

"Being in real estate, she knows a lot of people

around here, including the Lovelys." Donna glanced out my kitchen window at Peyton as she ran by with Fozzie. "In fact, she was telling me how Kevin Lovely came on to her last year."

"Really." If this was true, I wondered if this was before or after Scarlett started working for him.

"Personally, I think she was embellishing. You remember how competitive she was with Heather back in high school."

What I remembered was how things got catty after Crystal didn't get enough votes to make the cheer squad. The rumor was that had been Heather's doing—a rumor I had always assumed that Crystal started since I didn't vote for her either.

"Not much has changed. She's still determined to one-up the rest of us." Donna smiled with satisfaction, adding, "She just has much better hair now."

"I'm sure she does." Crystal always looked groomed like a polished and highly successful professional in the promotional flyers I received at the house each month. She also looked like she'd had a nose job.

"You should talk to her."

I wasn't thrilled with the idea, but I didn't disagree.

Plus, it would give me an opportunity to see what other work she'd had done. "Fine. Do you have her number?"

"I do. Not only that, I can send you her address in Port Townsend."

Within a minute I had a text from Donna, which I read while she called out to Peyton that it was time to go home.

After a quick goodbye hug and an assurance that I'd see Donna next Saturday for that haircut I needed, I walked the girls out to their car. Then I headed back inside to change my clothes.

I had another trip to Port Townsend to make.

Chapter Twenty-One

An hour and a half later, I had bypassed downtown Port Townsend and was driving west into farm country on Hastings Avenue when the automated voice of my navigation app instructed me to make a left turn in a quarter mile.

Slowing, I looked for a road. The only thing ahead on the left that came close was a narrow stretch of dirt cut through the center of an alfalfa field.

"Turn left."

"Here?" There was no road sign—no sign of any kind to indicate that this dirt driveway was Ida Lane.

"Turn left," the disembodied voice repeated. "Then your destination will be on the left."

"Seriously?" She sounded way too confident about that.

This so-called lane barely looked wide enough for the tractor necessary to work these fields, and there was no house in sight. Just a copse of tall trees off in the distance.

I pulled over to the shoulder and opened the browser

on my phone to verify Zack Wooten's address.

With no cell towers for miles, the people-finder website took a while to load, but after a minute it confirmed the Port Townsend address I had written down when I ran his background check: 101 Ida Lane.

It also listed an Ida Wooten as having lived at this address along with Bruce Wooten, Martha Blaisdell Wooten, and Chastity Wooten.

Okay, not a wrong address. Just a hard to find one.

I slipped my phone back into the pocket of the black blazer I'd worn so that I could look the part for the cover story I'd planned on using.

It was straight from an episode of *Peachtree Girls*, Marietta's old show. I didn't have the horn-rimmed glasses that she had worn when she went undercover as a private investigator's assistant. But I had made liberal use of my best felt tip liquid liner to create a dramatic cat eye, paired that with some smoky shadow, applied false eyelashes, and had painted my lips a glossy cherry red.

After a dusting of powder to eliminate a few freckles, I looked like a cross between *His Girl Friday* and *Elvira, Mistress of the Dark*.

As long as I didn't look like my usual self, I was good with that.

Getting out of my car, I walked across the street. Brisk gusts of wind blew my overly long bangs into my eyes and made me regret that I hadn't used more hairspray to hold the bun at the nape of my neck in place.

Or brought some with me so that I could fix my hair.

Best-laid plans this was not. I wasn't even sure I was in the right place.

Pushing strands of my hair out of my face, I noticed a mailbox hiding under a swaying branch of a fir tree growing near the road. Upon closer inspection I saw three bullet holes in the side of the mailbox, giving it the same abandoned appearance as the dilapidated fruit stand I had passed five minutes earlier.

But I found what I had been seeking.

Drilled into the rusting length of pipe propping up the mailbox was a green metal sign with white lettering: *Ida Lane.*

It also appeared to have been used for target practice.

I had visited enough remote locations on the peninsula where I had grown up to know that this was par for the course. Mailboxes were easy targets out here, as were road signs. The few bordering the county roads where there were more cows than people were typically riddled with bullet holes.

Probably kids, out joyriding with a case of beer and a loaded weapon, which was as good as asking for trouble. But cows didn't tend to complain.

Yep, this area was pretty darn remote, I thought as I scanned my surroundings. I didn't even see any cows.

There were three horses grazing in the field across the way, but if Zack lived here, and if he were home, and if he didn't take kindly to my visit, I knew I couldn't count on any of them to come galloping to my aid if things went sideways.

That added up to a whole lot of *ifs.*

Then I added one more. Because *if* I hadn't already had the niggling feeling that I should think twice about the wisdom of interviewing Zack Wooten at his home instead of a public place, I had it in spades now.

"Nope," I said, heading back to my car. This was definitely not anywhere close to a good plan. "No one even knows where I am."

The phone in my pocket rang as if someone had been listening in. Or watching.

With my pulse spiking as I reached for my phone, I took another look around while the breeze whipped tendrils of hair into my face. Same horses, a vehicle off in the distance, a couple of crows hanging out on a power line fifty feet away. Nothing that signaled danger.

Clearly, I needed to rein in my imagination, especially since I could see by the caller ID that this was just Crystal Zimmerman returning my call.

So, cool it with the niggling.

I had hoped that the message I left her an hour earlier would have made me sound like a hot prospect. So hot that she'd want to find some time for me this afternoon.

And it just so happened that I now had the time.

"Hello," I said, trying to sound natural as I hurried into my car and locked the door.

I heard no reply.

"Hello?"

There was nothing but the beeping sound of a dropped call.

I looked down at my phone. No service.

"What the heck!"

Scrambling out of my car, I walked up the road to see if I could find a signal, away from the squawking crows that seemed to be mocking me for being such a nervous nelly and toward a faded red barn on the other side of the alfalfa field.

Still no bars.

Holding my phone skyward, I turned in a circle as if I were praying to the cellular gods. And maybe my prayers were answered because it started ringing.

"Let's try this again, shall we?" Crystal jokingly said after we exchanged hellos.

"Sorry, I'm in the middle of nowhere, looking at a property." Which was conveniently true. It just didn't happen to be for sale. "The reception is horrible here."

"It's not much better here, so I'll make this fast in case I lose you."

Fine with me. I wanted to talk to her in person, not on the phone.

"I have to say though what a nice surprise it was to hear from you," Crystal continued with a friendly lilt to her voice. "Why I was just telling Donna yesterday that we should all get together. It's been too long."

I suspected that she was testing the waters to find out if I had chatted with Donna in the last twenty-four hours.

"Way too long." I didn't want to weaken my excuse for calling her, so I didn't volunteer any additional information. "That's why you were the first person I thought of when my mom mentioned that she was interested in investing in some rental properties. I'm acting as her representative. You know, doing the legwork so that she can maintain a low profile." Extremely low since Marietta knew nothing about this. "And I wanted to go with an agent I could trust."

"Well, I'm very glad you thought of me."

When she didn't suggest meeting for coffee or drinks, I figured that was my cue to let her know I was in town.

"She was thinking one or two vacation rentals in Port Townsend to start with. I drove by one I found online, but like I said, it's out in the middle of nowhere." I added a sigh for dramatic effect. "Not exactly a vacation destination."

"You're in Port Townsend now?" Crystal asked.

"More like the outskirts but I was going to head into town to get one of those real estate brochures before I headed home."

"Don't bother. Those listings are so old they're a complete waste of your time. Why don't you come to the office instead."

Exactly what I wanted to hear. "Oh, okay."

"I'm on Harstone Island wrapping up an open house, but I should be back by four if that works for you."

"That works just fine." Very much so.

"Great! I'll text you the address."

Walking toward my car, I checked the time on my phone after we disconnected. It was almost three, so I had a little over an hour to kill. Maybe I could find someplace to get out of the wind and fix my hair. Tone down the makeup, too.

Not that I was overly concerned about how I came

across to Crystal. I knew that the prospect of earning a fat commission was all my former classmate would care about.

I was much more concerned about the tortilla beige Toyota pickup that was slowly rolling toward me.

Crap.

The crows squawked as if they were members of the neighborhood watch, urging me to rush to the safety of my Subaru.

I would have if I could, but the pickup stopped, blocking my path.

Double crap.

The window rolled down and the older woman behind the wheel smiled. "You lost, honey?"

The pulse that had been racing in my ears throttled back toward a normal rhythm when I saw she was the lone occupant of the truck. "No, I'm good. Thanks."

"'Cause if you're lookin' for someone who lives in these parts, I could probably point you in the right direction."

She had a tan, freckled face, a graying copper mop of hair, and dark eyes behind slightly tinted glasses. There were a few fine lines around her unpainted lips with many more etched into her brow. Even though she looked a good ten years older than my mother, I had a feeling that their birthdays weren't that far apart.

I didn't get any off-putting vibes from the woman, so I decided to take her up on her offer. "Do you know the Wootens?"

"Yeah, I know 'em," she said after a beat of hesitation.

I pointed behind me. "Is their house back there somewhere?"

"If you don't mind me asking, who wants to know?"

I didn't want to give her my name. "It's a private matter."

Narrowing her eyes, she muttered an obscenity. "What's he done this time?"

I didn't want to make more trouble for Zack Wooten than he was already in. I was about to apologize for giving her the wrong impression about why I was here when she waved me off.

"Never mind. I don't need the aggravation. Come on back if you wanna talk to him." She rolled up her window and turned onto Ida Lane, kicking up a cloud of dust that the wind promptly blew in my direction.

I could stand there and eat her dust, or I could make a run for my car.

Some decisions aren't very tough.

I then had another decision to make after I slid behind the wheel.

"You gonna do this or what?" I asked as I smoothed back my hair in the rearview mirror.

It was the reason I'd made the trip out here, and now I knew someone else would be around if I needed help— probably Martha, Zack's mother.

Nothing to worry about, right?

"Right," I muttered, wishing that I felt more convinced.

But Zack's mom hadn't impressed me as someone who would let anything bad happen under her roof. And

Zack didn't have a history of violence.

"So let's get this over with."

Starting the ignition, I made the left turn before I changed my mind and followed the pickup down the rutted lane past several tall fir trees to a century-old, two-story farmhouse that looked like it hadn't been painted since the Clinton administration. Still, it had a rustic charm with cornflower blue shutters, a banana-yellow front door, and a thin trail of smoke escaping a brick chimney. Two wicker chairs sat on the wooden porch to the right of the door. Behind the chairs, a shaggy white dog the size of my grandmother's tabby cat stood at attention in the picture window.

As soon as I parked next to the Toyota and opened my door, the woman stepped out from behind her truck with a grocery bag in her arms while the dog barked an intruder alert.

"Zack's in there," she stated flatly, gesturing with her chin toward the creamsicle mobile home on blocks at the end of the dirt driveway, where a faded red Mustang was parked.

"Okay, thanks." Buttoning my blazer over the ivory blouse I typically wore when I was needed in court, I watched her disappear through a side door of the house.

So much for Zack's mother being under the same roof.

At least she'd be next door and I heard a guy telling the dog to shut up, so someone else was around, maybe her husband. Which was about as good of a situation as I could ask for, considering the circumstances.

"In and out. Fifteen minutes, tops," I promised myself as I walked toward the single-wide mobile home in relative quiet now that I was out of the yappy dog's line of sight.

Climbing the three steps up to the aluminum door, I sucked in a deep breath, straightened my shoulders, and knocked.

It was showtime.

I heard what sounded like an announcer for a football game and someone moving inside. Seconds later, the door swung open on squeaky hinges and the twenty-three-year-old I recognized from his social media posts stared down at me.

Zack Wooten was taller than I'd thought. Close to Steve's height, around six feet, but maybe twenty pounds lighter. Freckles dotted a straight, longish nose and a few acne scars pitted the hollows of his cheeks. His jawline was covered in patchwork ruddy stubble, making him look like a guy who couldn't grow a decent beard. Like his mother, he had shaggy layers of honey-red hair and dark eyes, but that was where the resemblance stopped. He didn't have her tan or the squint lines of someone who worked outdoors.

Zack also didn't have her ability to make a good first impression, especially since he smelled like he'd been marinating in a keg of beer. Maybe last night's keg, based on his bedhead and the rumpled T-shirt he'd probably slept in.

"Zack Wooten?" I politely asked.

His brow furrowed as if he couldn't decide if this were

my everyday look or if I was a month late with my Halloween costume. "Yeah?"

"I'm Nina with Salsiccia Investigations," I said, pausing after the first syllable of my favorite kind of Italian sausage to make it sound like the name Saul.

According to my Google search, there were no Sauls working as PIs on the peninsula, so if Zack wanted to verify my story later, he wouldn't get very far. And I was pretty dang sure he wouldn't be able to spell Salsiccia.

Rubbing a hand over one of his eyes, he yawned. "You're who?"

Since the guy looked hungover, maybe I didn't need to worry about him entering any spelling bees today.

"My name's Nina," I said, borrowing the name my mother always used when she worked undercover in *Peachtree Girls*. "I work for Saul. We've been hired to find witnesses to a hit and run that took place in town earlier this month. May I come in?"

Zack shook his head. "I don't know nothin' about a hit and run."

I was expecting that he'd say something like that since I had made up the story shortly after I left my house.

I flashed him an encouraging smile. "Another witness placed you near the scene, so you may know more than you think. Please, may I come in to ask you a couple of questions?"

"I guess." After raking a hand through his hair as if he thought he should make himself presentable for female company, Zack held the door open for me.

I entered a wood-paneled living room with stained carpet the color of burnt toast. The enclosed space reeked of cigarette smoke and garbage that should have been dumped weeks ago. If I hadn't known better, I would have sworn that I was downwind of a landfill.

Bamboo blinds hung at a slant, mostly covering a window behind a sagging tweedy sofa. Next to it, a frosted light fixture coated with at least twenty years of grime hung from a brass chain. A laptop sat on a wooden crate facing the sofa with the volume up high enough to hear down the length of the dark-paneled hallway to my right.

Stepping around the empty beer cans that didn't make it into the plastic waste basket next to the door, I heard voices I recognized from years of watching Sunday football with my grandfather. Two network regulars were debating the wisdom of putting in a rookie quarterback, which made it sound like I might have arrived during a break in the action.

I turned to Zack. "Sorry if I'm interrupting the game."

Kicking aside the cans in his path, he slapped the laptop shut. "It's half-time. Thirty-one to zip, so the game's pretty much over already."

When he dropped onto one end of the sofa, I figured I was supposed to do the same, especially since there was nowhere else to sit. But that was okay because this gave me the close proximity I needed to get a good read of Zack's face. Plus, the natural light seeping through the blinds made my only option a fairly well-lit one.

I just needed to keep my cool and not think about what might be crawling under my butt.

Pulling my notebook and a pen from my tote, I perched at the edge of a lumpy seat cushion so that I could face him.

"I'll get right to the point," I said, clicking my pen to signal the start of the interview. "We have a witness who stated that you were seen near the location of a hit and run that occurred on Sims Way on..." I checked my notes for dramatic effect. "November seventh. That would have been a Saturday night."

Zack frowned. "Whaddya mean, I was seen?"

"Just that. You were seen by someone who was in the area, and—"

"I didn't have anything to do with that! And if someone says I did, they don't know what they're talkin' about." Sinking back into the sofa, he hung his head and folded his tattooed arms like a child given a time-out, only this child had well-developed biceps.

Obviously, beer cans weren't the only things he lifted.

"Sir, no one's accusing you of anything," I assured him. "We're just trying to find witnesses to this accident."

"I already told you. I didn't see nothin'."

"If you'll indulge me, let's retrace your steps that night so that we can eliminate you from our witness list."

Zack shrugged.

I referred to my notebook where I had written the convenience store name and approximate time that Heather said she and Kevin Lovely were there. "Were you, in fact, at the Speedy Mart on Sims Way the night of November seventh? It would have been around nine."

Instead of answering, he reached for the phone in the pocket of his worn jeans.

I was close enough to see that he was scrolling through his text messages.

Zack must have found the one he was looking for because he leaned back to pocket the phone. "Yeah, so?"

"Did you see or hear anything unusual happening on the street?"

"Nope."

"Were you there alone?"

"Yeah, I went in for some smokes," he said in the easy manner of someone accustomed to bending uncomfortable truths. "I was out."

That last part was a common tell—extra information to sell the lie.

"That may be true." Given the collection of butts in the ashtray next to the laptop, I didn't doubt that he might have gone into the store while he was waiting for Kevin Lovely to show up. "But that's not the reason you went there that night, right?"

Zack's dark eyes widened. With better light I probably could have seen his pupils constrict, which would have been another tell. "Huh?"

"You were seen meeting with someone." I checked my notes again as if I were unfamiliar with the name. "He's been identified as Kevin Lovely."

"Yeah, I…uh…ran into him in the parking lot when I was coming out of the store."

Close enough. If I challenged Zack on every little aspect of his story, I was afraid he'd clam up on me.

But I needed him to realize that he couldn't "bend" his way out of our conversation. "That's not quite the way your encounter with him was described. I was told that you gave him something."

Zack blinked, his jaw slack.

Gotcha.

"I don't care what it was," I stated with a nonchalance that I hoped disguised the fact I was dying to know. "And I'm not trying to jam you up. But if this was a drug buy—"

"It wasn't." Leaning forward as if he could see more legal trouble coming to his door, Zack shook his head. "It was nothin' like that."

"I'm just saying that if it were like that, and you just happened to be hanging out in that parking lot to sell something to the hit and run driver—"

"I wasn't! I was just there to give Kevin somethin'."

Okay, now we were getting somewhere.

"Uh-huh." I injected a healthy dose of skepticism into my tone to see what else he'd volunteer. "Really, if it was coke for some party he was having, I don't care."

"It wasn't. It was just a letter."

"A letter." This wasn't what I had expected to hear, but I hadn't detected any signs of deception. Instead, the intensity with which Zack's gaze held mine felt earnest. A little desperate, too.

"You know, in an envelope."

Yeah, I knew what a letter was. "But you were seen taking something in exchange."

"It was money. But it wasn't for me."

I gave him another doubtful look. "Oh?"

"Really, it was for the baby."

As in Scarlett's baby?

"My fiancée's pregnant," he said.

"Your fiancée?" Based on what Sofia had told me, I had a hard time believing that Scarlett would want to marry this guy.

"Well, I'm hopin' she'll say yes. I asked when she came home for a Halloween party one of our friends was having. That's actually when she gave me the letter for Kevin." Zack lowered his voice as if he didn't want to admit this part. "He's the father."

Just like Heather got me to deliver her letter to Steve. Who knew that Kevin Lovely's lady friends would have so much in common?

"Just a letter in this envelope?" I asked to find out what all he knew about it.

"I guess. I didn't look. It was somethin' between her and him."

"Okay." I scribbled in my notebook as if Zack had provided me with all the pertinent details I needed. Which, in fact, he had. "And that's it? You didn't see or hear any car being driven recklessly on Sims Way?"

"Nah, I never heard nothin' about a hit and run, so I can't help you."

"And unfortunately, it seems that Mr. Lovely passed away from an untimely accident, so..." I left the sentence unfinished so that I could observe Zack's reaction.

"Yeah, that was crazy. Scarlett—that's my girlfriend's name. She was real shaken up when she heard about it."

"I can imagine." Especially since I'd heard the same thing from Sofia.

Zack smiled, the first one I'd seen since I arrived. "Guess Kevin can't be one of your witnesses."

I didn't make anything out of his wisecrack. He had probably thought he was being funny. A bit dark, but I'd heard a lot worse from the cop I was engaged to.

I'd also heard enough to be convinced that Zack had nothing to do with Kevin Lovely's death.

I smiled back. "Is she doing okay? Your girlfriend and the baby?"

"Yeah, we're all good." He nodded with a cocky assurance, but I suspected Scarlett wouldn't be so quick to agree with him.

Zack had probably been a very willing shoulder for her to cry on the last few months. As high school sweethearts, they had a past. And despite what Sofia told me about her cousin dumping this guy, he must have wriggled his way back into her heart. At least to some degree if he proposed. Time would tell if they had a future.

The safer bet would be on him serving time as a single man.

I snapped my notebook shut and then remembered that I had one lingering question for Zack.

"One last thing." Pulling out my cell phone, I showed him the picture from Jonah Lovely's basketball game. "Do you recognize this guy?"

Zack shook his head. "Is he involved in the hit and run?"

"He's just a person of interest." My interest.

Chapter Twenty-Two

Using my navigation app to find the address Crystal texted me, I was able to avoid waterfront area traffic by taking residential side streets and made good time. Just not good enough to do much about my makeup when I made a quick detour into the Port Townsend public library at three forty-five to use the restroom.

Again, this wasn't an example of best-laid plans, but it gave me a chance to wash my hands and get Zack Wooten's trailer stink off me. Plus, I really needed to pee.

I applied some fresh lip gloss, smoothed back the loose strands of my hair, and had to call it good enough if I didn't want to be late.

After I scrambled back into my car, I took the next left and drove past several modest homes to the corner, where I saw the Zimmerman Real Estate sign planted in the middle of a well-manicured front yard bordered by a short rock wall.

"Arrived," the app informed me as I pulled up next to the strip of grass growing between the sidewalk and the street.

This time I didn't need it to tell me the obvious. "I know."

Stepping out of my car, I shrugged out of my blazer so that I wouldn't look like I'd dressed for a business meeting. Then, I slung my tote over my shoulder and headed toward the walkway of a beautifully renovated two-story sage green bungalow with white trim and four porch columns that stretched from their brick bases to the shingled roof overhang.

Since every blade of grass in front of her place of business was clear of the rusty brown leaves covering the rest of the neighborhood like a dirty blanket, I assumed that Crystal hired someone to do regular yard maintenance.

It was also the greenest lawn in the neighborhood. Like Donna reminded me a few hours earlier, Crystal had always seemed determined to be the best at everything.

Based on the showplace I was looking at, along with the pearly white Cadillac SUV parked in the driveway like an accessory to the house, not much had changed.

The front door opened as I approached, and Crystal gave me a friendly wave. "Howdy, stranger!"

Pasting a smile on my face, I held up my hand in greeting. "Hi. Nice place."

"Thanks! We like it."

We? Her staff? The other agents who worked with her? I never saw any other smiling faces on those flyers than hers. I didn't see any other cars parked nearby either, so I wasn't sure if we'd be alone inside or not. I had assumed it would just be the two of us, but she didn't give me any more time to think about that than the seconds it took me to climb the front steps.

And by then I was focusing on her new, not-so-turned-up nose.

Crystal Tweedy Zimmerman had definitely had a little work done.

"It's so good to see you," she said, pulling me close for a quick Shalimar-scented squeeze to her ample bosom.

Make that amplified bosom and *more* than a little work done.

"It's been forever." She hooked my arm to lead me to the door and then her hazel-eyed gaze swept over my face. "If I hadn't known it was you, I don't know that I would've even recognized you."

Since I had led Crystal to believe that I'd come to town to scope out properties, I had to give her a good reason why I looked like I'd made time for an extreme makeover.

"It's the price I pay for being my mother's daughter. When she makes appearances for her makeup line and needs a volunteer..." I used my free hand to point at my face. "A bit much, I know, but I thought it was kind of fun going around almost incognito today."

Releasing me, Crystal opened the door. "It's definitely a fun look."

She didn't believe that any more than I did, but I didn't care and entered what I assumed had been the home's living room.

A lovely Oriental rug in celery, vanilla and nutmeg tones covered the dark hardwood entry, separating a waiting area with a cushy loveseat, a baroque coffee table that probably predated the house, and two lemongrass-striped wingback chairs from the elegant executive desk to the right of the door.

The stone desk top gleamed like a giant agate under the low wattage of an antique brass bankers lamp. A fragrant bouquet of roses and mums sat on display instead of the usual framed photos and electronics one would expect in a typical office.

Watercolors depicting the historic mansions of Port Townsend hung on each wall, while a Victorian dollhouse sat in the corner on a console table below the white spindle staircase to the second floor.

With the decor of a well-appointed showroom, every inch of space screamed interior designer, unlike the mobile home I had just left that screamed for a fumigator.

"We can chat in my office," Crystal said, leading me to a large room opposite a kitchen where I could smell coffee brewing.

With glass double doors and a picture window covered by panels of lace, her office looked like a reimagined dining room, complete with a built-in china cabinet that she was using for books, awards, candles, framed photos of her husband and kids, and a Christmas cactus tipped with hot pink blooms.

Crystal pointed at the two high-back leather chairs facing her antique white executive desk. "Make yourself comfortable. Want some coffee?"

It smelled great and ordinarily I would have jumped at the chance to get a boost of caffeine, but I didn't want to encourage Crystal to hold a cup in front of her face and obscure my view.

"No thanks," I said, taking the closest seat. "A little late in the day for me."

"Herbal tea? Water?"

I waved her off. "No thanks, I'm good."

She stood at the edge of her tidy desk, looking tall and trim in a navy pinstriped suit and pumps. Gone were the saddlebags I remembered from high school. Gone was at least fifteen pounds, too. Either from diet or liposuction, or both.

A fluffy mahogany bob with cinnamon streaks framed her oval face. Donna was right. Crystal Zimmerman had good hair. And her makeup was subtle, perfectly professional, just like on her flyers.

Although I'd had a preview of what to expect, I hadn't expected her to look *this* good, and I couldn't help but feel a pang of envy.

"What?" she asked, her eyes wide.

Oops, she'd caught me staring.

"Oh." Crystal nodded as if she guessed what I had been thinking. "The nose, right?"

I shrugged. "I was just noticing—"

"I had it done years ago," she said as she sunk into her creamy leather desk chair. "Just shows how long it's been since we've seen one another."

"Well, you look great." Leaning back, I made a sweeping gesture worthy of a game show hostess. "And your office is lovely."

Crystal beamed. "Thanks! It took some renovation, but we're really happy with how it turned out."

There was that *we* again. "You have other agents that work with you here?"

"Just one, my husband, Rick. He handles the commercial side of the business."

I glanced toward the double doors that she hadn't closed. "If he's here, I'd love to meet him."

"No, he's home with the kids, so it's just us."

Good. The fewer interruptions the better.

"And if you don't mind," she added, kicking off her pumps. "After all day in these shoes, my feet are killing me."

I smiled sympathetically. "Hey, if I could go to work in fuzzy slippers, I would."

"Speaking of work, someone mentioned that you're a deputy coroner. Is that right? You're working for Frankie Rickard?"

Someone with a big mouth by the name of Donna, no doubt. "I'm deputized—almost all of us on her staff are—but I'm more like the department gopher. Nothing you'd be interested in." And not what I came here to talk about.

"Oh." Crystal pressed her lips together as if she'd hoped I had some beans to spill about a recent death. "I thought..."

Donna may not have known when to keep her mouth shut, but I did. Especially when the other person had more to say.

"Well, you know how rumors get around," Crystal said, giving her head a shake as if such things were beneath her.

"I do indeed." And could only hope that she wanted to talk about a rumor involving Kevin Lovely.

"I know it's not my place to ask, but I thought I heard that certain people think that Veronica Lovely had something to do with her husband's death."

Certain people? I didn't have to ask who Crystal was referring to.

"Don't believe everything you hear," I said.

Leaning back in her chair, she tapped an index finger against the armrest as if she were trying to decide what to believe: what I had just told her or what she had overheard in that alley yesterday.

Crystal stopped tapping. "I know her. We've spent time together."

"Who? Veronica?"

She nodded. "She and Kevin did such a great job for one of my clients a few years back that Rick and I used them when we remodeled our house. Heck, Veronica did all the interior design for this place. All I did was show her the watercolors I wanted to use, and she did all the rest."

None of this came as any surprise given what Donna had told me. Plus, I was pretty sure that Crystal hadn't found that dollhouse on her own. "She's good."

"He was good, too," she said on a sigh, staring at a pink lotus flower paperweight on the corner of her desk. "Really good...at everything."

Crystal looked as if she were conjuring up a memory in which Kevin might have removed his tool belt.

"That's what I've heard."

My tone dripped with so much innuendo that if she didn't react emotionally, she would have to be as dead inside as the guy we were talking about.

She blinked, a flush creeping into her cheeks. "What do you mean?"

"You know, the man had a reputation. And people around here talk." To say the least. "A pregnancy will do that."

Crystal blew out a breath as if she were relieved that I hadn't been referring to her. "Yeah, I was shocked to hear about the girl who worked there."

"I imagine Veronica was, too."

"I think she knew about his wandering eye. I mean, I did, so how could she not? Not to say anything happened with me." She casually flicked a wrist, but the action was at odds with the fake smile frozen at her lips. "Kevin was just a big flirt. At the time I thought it was totally harmless. I mean, who doesn't mind turning a handsome man's head?"

I had no doubt that something happened after that head was turned, but that wasn't what I had come here to find out.

"That's pretty much what my mother said after the Lovelys came over to consult on a kitchen project—that he was a charming flirt."

"He was charming, for sure."

"And she was really impressed with them as a team,"

I added to see if Crystal had anything else to say on that subject.

She nodded. "They made a great team."

All she was doing was agreeing with me. I needed to approach this from another angle.

"I heard there were talks about them being featured in a home improvement show." I didn't dare mention my source.

"Really! That's news to me."

"It could just be one of those rumors floating around, but now that half the team is gone..."

"Still, Veronica might be able to pull it off. Maybe after she's had time to think about what she wants to do with the business. Certainly, after she's had time to mourn."

Given how eager Veronica had seemed to continue the talks with my mother, I wasn't so sure about that last part.

"Then again, it could just be the latest rumor to hit Duke's Cafe," I said. "Like the one about the guy she was seen with a few days ago."

Crystal's gaze sharpened. "What guy?"

"I don't know. Some big, hunky guy. Oh, I almost forgot. One of the waitresses sent me a picture." Confident that I was the only one of the two of us who knew I was lying, I retrieved my phone from my tote and pretended to search through my texts.

"Here it is. This is the guy," I said, reaching across Crystal's desk to show her the mystery hunk's picture.

She squinted at it and then smiled as if she were in

the catbird seat. "Tell your waitress friend that this is nothing. They're family."

"What, like he's her brother or something?" Because there was no family resemblance.

"No, on Kevin's side—a cousin, I think. I met him when Veronica and I went to him with a chair I wanted reupholstered. Nice guy. A bit slow to warm up, but he does really good work. Must be a talent that runs in the family."

"I have an old loveseat that needs some new upholstery." Which happened to be true. I just hadn't given any serious thought to updating it until she mentioned the cousin's line of work. "What's his name?"

"Will? No, that doesn't sound right. What was his name?" Crystal opened a desk drawer. "I know I took one of his business cards." She removed a rubber band and sorted through the inch-thick stack of cards with the efficiency of a Vegas dealer. "Here it is. Wyatt McGowan."

"May I see that? I'll snap a picture of it so that I have his contact info."

A second later, I aimed my camera phone at a plain white business card with *McGowan & Son Furniture Restoration* embossed in black. Since "Serving our customers since 1990" was centered in the space below the Port Townsend address, I assumed Wyatt was the son.

I handed the card back to Crystal. "Thanks, I'll definitely follow up with him." Most definitely.

Instead of returning the card to the stack where she had found it, Crystal blinked down at it.

"What?" I asked, hoping that she had remembered

something else from her visit to Wyatt McGowan's shop.

"I was just thinking about the couples they feature on those home improvement shows. They aren't always a real couple; sometimes they're just business associates."

I nodded, my pulse quickening as I anticipated where Crystal was going with this.

"Business associates where one is the idea person—someone with an eye for design like Veronica. And the other person is the master craftsman who's going to say it can't be done but always manages to pull it off by the end of the episode." The corners of Crystal's mouth lifted as she toyed with the business card in her hand. "Wyatt would fit that bill perfectly. He knows the business, especially when it comes to restoring the Victorians around here and all the woodwork inside of them. And, of course, he's a total hottie."

I wasn't sure how to respond to that. "Not everyone wants to be on TV and have cameras invading their space."

"But it could be a great way to get the name of his business out there. That's the approach I'd take if I were Veronica and needed a partner for a home improvement show."

"When you put it that way, it makes sense. Still, it's a big decision, and if he's got a wife working with him and kids, he might not want them—"

"No wife, no kids." She winked. "I asked, just out of curiosity."

Curiosity.

Just an innocent question about the total hottie.

Right.

I forced a smile. "Then he could be the perfect partner. *If* there really is a TV show in the works, and *if* Veronica could talk him into doing it."

"Oh, please." Crystal waved the business card at me. "I've seen her in action. Heck, she talked me into this antique desk. Do you know how much it cost?" I got another wave. "Never mind. You don't want to know. Just trust me. That woman can be very persuasive."

Persuasive enough to convince Wyatt McGowan to kill his cousin?

Chapter Twenty-Three

Monday morning, I rolled into the courthouse parking lot to the sound of my cell phone dinging with a text message.

It didn't stop dinging until I stepped onto the checkerboard tile of the third-floor landing. By then, I had received six text messages. All of them from Crystal.

I cringed, hating that I was wasting her time. Hating that I needed to provide some sort of a response, too.

"Oh, what a tangled web we weave," I muttered, opening her first text, which included a link for a Water Street townhome that had just hit the listing service and was "priced to sell" at a million dollars and change.

This was priced to sell? Sheesh!

The next five were to let me know about waterfront homes in Port Merritt and on Whidbey Island, each one billed as the perfect getaway location. And each more expensive than the last.

"Not where I told you to look and way over budget," I grumbled, getting increasingly annoyed at how my bogus vacation rental hunt was going.

I thought about calling Crystal to say as much, but the sheriff's deputy working security at his desk opposite the stairs was looking equally annoyed, folding his arms across his burly chest.

The two courtrooms he sat between wouldn't be in session for another hour, but his message couldn't be more clear: Keep it down.

Fine. I didn't want to talk to her anyway.

I stepped toward the yellow vinyl chairs lining the wall across from the county prosecutor's office door to send a quick text.

"I'll let you know if my mother is interested in any of these."

It was a little terse, but it was consistent with what I said yesterday, after Crystal made printouts of her top vacation rental prospects to take home with me.

I figured that should be my standard reply to each hot prospect she sent me, at least for the next week. After that, I'd tell Crystal that my mother's accountant wanted her to rethink her investment strategy and then apologize for the abrupt change of plans.

Did I feel awful to waste Crystal's time by sending her on this wild goose chase?

Absolutely.

But since she had been able to identify Wyatt McGowan, did I feel like my devious ends justified the means?

Absolutely.

But it also felt like each ding of my phone was karma with a message for me.

You created this wild goose chase, now enjoy the ride.

Ding.

I didn't bother to check. I knew who it was from. Just as I was more convinced than ever that karma was a bitch.

Instead, I turned on my phone's Do Not Disturb feature to silence her for the next few minutes and pushed open the heavy oak door to my right.

After greeting the receptionist, I headed down the hall to see if Patsy had anything pressing for me to do before I settled into my usual morning routine.

Patsy Faraday was Frankie's long-time legal assistant and sat outside of her office like a sentry, her sharp gray eyes missing nothing. Since she was my unofficial supervisor, this included my comings and goings.

"Good morning," I said when she stopped clicking on her keyboard long enough to acknowledge my presence.

Patsy's gaze slanted to the glass-domed anniversary clock ticking next to her computer monitor prior to looking up at me like a disapproving headmistress. "Good morning."

After two years of working with this woman, I had grown accustomed to starting my day this way. Whether I was late or five minutes early, like I was this morning, her reaction would be the same.

Having worked under some head chefs who used fear and intimidation to keep the staff in line, this daily dollop of condescension was nothing. Just Patsy's way of reminding me of the pecking order.

Bless her condescending heart.

"Anything interesting going on?" Frankie's office was dark, so I assumed that something had delayed the arrival of the boss we shared, not that Patsy would divulge any information to me. Everything was always on a need-to-know basis with her. Still, it didn't hurt to ask.

"Always." Patsy reached behind her for a thin stack of manila folders, a wry smile lifting the corners of her fleshy mouth. "Some *interesting* filing for you."

Swell.

"Okay." That would keep me busy for ten minutes at the most.

"That's all for now," she said, effectively banishing me from her sight.

Also okay. I had a background check I was itching to run and hightailed it to my desk.

Over the next four hours, I caught up on the filing, sat in on a witness interview, made five pots of coffee, helped Jan with a research project, and used the rest of my time to conduct a research project of my own. A pretty fruitless one given what little I found out about Wyatt McGowan.

He was forty-three, served four years as a Marine after high school, and then came back home to Port Townsend to work for his father. No wife and no kids, confirming what Crystal had told me. Also, no arrests and no warrants.

In fact, no criminal history of any kind.

"How can a guy look so badass and be so squeaky clean?" I asked while I typed his name into a search engine.

McGowan had no social media presence that I could find. He owned a house in Port Townsend, had two vehicles and a motorcycle registered in his name, and his business reputation seemed solid with scores of positive reviews.

There was nothing to indicate that he was anything less than a model citizen.

Nothing yet, anyway.

"Karla and I are heading out for lunch," Jan said, approaching my desk.

Startled by her sudden appearance, I immediately closed the search window and pasted a smile on my face.

"Want to join us?" She glanced at the open notebook in front of me. "Or are you in the middle of something?"

"No, I was just looking up upholsterers in the area. Someone recommended McGowan's. Have you heard anything about that place?" I figured that would give me cover if she had seen the name.

Jan nodded. "It's probably the only one around here that I know anything about, and that's only because I tagged along with my sister when she decided to recover the living room furniture her kids brutalized. I don't know if he's the owner, but the guy who does all the upholstery work? Honey, I thought I was gonna have to wipe the drool from Leanne's mouth."

"That impressive, huh?"

"I know you're engaged, but you should go just to check him out," Jan said.

"I may just have to do that." With any luck before he

closed tonight.

Wearing the hooded rain slicker she'd had on when she arrived around eleven-thirty, Karla stood in front of her desk and shot us an impatient glare. "Are you coming? I'm starving."

The steely gray layers that typically curled over Karla's ears stuck out in pointy chunks worthy of a punk rocker, evidence of her morning spent in the windy drizzle.

While helping Jan earlier, I had already heard that Frankie had called Karla out to where a body had been found near Clatska, so I didn't need to ask where she had been. But I was curious to hear the details of what she had seen and didn't hesitate to grab my coat.

By the time Jan, Karla, and I were seated at a booth along the rear wall of the Roadkill Grill, I had heard enough about the motorcyclist found near a dead deer to understand how Karla had wrapped up her investigation before lunch. Also why I hadn't been asked to assist.

Similar to the circumstances surrounding Kevin Lovely's death, Frankie had been quick to agree with the county sheriff's investigator that Tyler Neuberger had landed down a tree-lined slope off State Route 17 because of an accident. Only this time, there had first been a collision with a deer.

There had been no eyewitnesses in this densely wooded area outside of Clatska to interview. The early morning jogger who had spotted the motorcycle with his headlamp lived over a mile away and hadn't heard anything. Tyler's parents, who had reported the twenty-year-old missing when he didn't come home last night, had insisted to Karla that their son wasn't a drug user or a drinker.

Before she left the scene, Frankie had arranged for Tyler's fluids to be sent to the state crime lab, so in around six weeks we would have confirmation if his parents had been right. In the meantime, there was just a deer to blame along with a skid mark to indicate where it had been standing in the road.

Once our food arrived, it was clear that Karla wanted to focus on her egg salad sandwich instead of the sad details that would soon go into her report.

At least her report should be quick to write.

Heck, there were so many similarities to how Kevin Lovely's car took a nosedive into a tree near his house, Karla could copy the report she had written last week and simply change a few salient details.

The names and addresses.

The dead deer.

The fact that there had been no eyewitness to last night's accident. No neighbors in this remote area to see or hear anything.

Which made me wonder what the Lovelys' neighbors had seen that day.

Chapter Twenty-Four

After sliding behind the wheel of my car shortly after five and firing up the heater, I plucked my cell phone from my tote to ask Steve if he wanted to go out to dinner and saw that I had missed two calls from him.

Not only that, but I had also received five texts: one from Steve, one from Marietta, and three from Crystal.

"Dang it!" I still had my phone in Do Not Disturb mode. Easy enough to fix, but no wonder I hadn't heard a peep out of it since this morning.

While raindrops coated my windshield, I read Steve's text and was relieved to see that it had nothing to do with any death, injury, or relative who was coming for a surprise visit. He was simply letting me know that he was going to help cover for Eddie while he worked on a couple of pinsetters that had been jamming all day.

Since Steve would be compensated for his time with all the pizza he could eat, I texted back that he should bring me home a slice along with a side salad.

With dinner covered, I read my mother's message. Twice. It didn't make any more sense the second time since she had inserted so many abbreviations and emojis that it would require a decoder ring for me to decipher. But seeing Veronica's name in the same sentence as a wineglass emoji told me I had better find out what this was about.

I put my phone on speaker as I pulled out of the courthouse parking lot and was relieved to hear Marietta pick up on the second ring.

"About time," she said with no trace of her irritating fake accent but making up for it with an infusion of tone. "Is your day so busy that you don't have time for a quick conversation with your mother?"

No conversation with my mother was ever quick, but since I had a forty-minute drive to Port Townsend ahead of me, I had the time now.

"Sorry, I was in meetings most of the afternoon," I said, bending the truth. "I read your text. Want to translate it for me?"

"What's to translate? Veronica and I are going to discuss the show over drinks tomorrow."

That explained the wineglass emoji, but it sure wasn't what I wanted to hear. "I thought you were going to give her some time to figure out how she wanted to move forward without her husband."

"Apparently, she doesn't need the time because she's the one who contacted me."

Yeah, that wasn't the least bit suspicious. "Okay."

"So, are you available?"

"You want me to go with you?" Why?

"It should have been clear from my text. I want you to

drive me."

And that explained the car emoji.

But I still didn't understand, especially now that she had a fancy new Mercedes. "Weren't you just saying how you could see just fine in the dark and no longer need me to be your chauffeur?"

Marietta released a sigh. "I had a little accident."

"How little? Are you okay?"

"I'm fine, but the Mercedes is going to be in the shop for a few days."

"You've only had that car for two weeks. What the heck happened?"

"My foot slipped and..." Marietta said hesitantly, her words trailing off into an unintelligible mumble.

"I didn't catch that. What?"

There was a long silence in which I could almost hear her grinding her teeth. "I said my foot slipped, and I hit the gas instead of the brake."

Given the damage to her car, this couldn't have been the whole story. "And what did you run into?"

"Nothing major. Just the garage."

"You mean the garage door?"

"A teensy bit more than just the door. A contractor is going to come out Wednesday and give us an estimate."

Good grief. Mayhem Moreau had struck again.

"Anyhoo, enough about my little mishap. Are you available tomorrow?"

For another chance to observe Veronica up close and personal? "Sure. As long as it's after work."

"That won't be a problem. We're meeting at six at the

Bayside."

Steve and I had eaten at that waterfront bistro a handful of times. Unlike most of the restaurants near Old Town, it had ample parking, making the Bayside a popular after-work watering hole.

"The bar fills up fast, so you might want to get there earlier to grab a table," I said.

"Actually, I thought the bar might be too loud, so I made a reservation in the restaurant—a nice, quiet table for four."

"Four? Who else is coming?"

"You'll never believe this. Do you remember the hunk of a man we saw sitting next to Veronica at the game?"

All too well. "Yep."

"Well, we sure were wrong to judge that book by its cover." Marietta chuckled. "Guess what he does."

I didn't need to guess. "What?"

"He restores antiques! Actually, all kinds of furniture. Does upholstery, too. Veronica says he can fix anything. She's been working with him for years. Turns out they're family, which is ideal for the show. You know, for the on-camera banter to feel natural. And with the way he looks, all tall, dark, and studly, he couldn't be a more perfect partner for her!"

"Yeah, perfect," I muttered, slowing to take the next left off Main Street since there was no longer any point in my leaving town to talk with the guy.

While my mother continued to sing the praises of a man she didn't know, having taken the word of a woman she barely knew, whose cheating husband died under suspicious circumstances, I headed home.

"Did Veronica say that she's talked to him about this?" I asked when Marietta finally paused to take a breath.

"She hasn't gone into any detail with him. We're gonna do that tomorrow evening. I think all she's told him so far is that she has a business opportunity for him."

Then, unless this meeting was being staged for my mother's benefit, I should be able to see some indication of surprise on Wyatt McGowan's face.

"And Charmaine, I want you to treat this like a business meeting, so please wear something appropriate."

No one was going to be looking at me, not while I sat next to Port Merritt's one and only celebrity. "Yes, Mother."

"Now, don't get snippy. I just want to make a good impression on the man, especially since we didn't seem to start off on the right foot last Friday."

"I'm sure it will go fine," I said, even though I wasn't sure of anything where Veronica Lovely was concerned.

"From your lips to God's ears 'cause I really want this to go well. See you tomorrow?"

"I'll be there." Absolutely, positively.

Two hours later, I was finishing a bowl of instant oatmeal in front of the TV when Fozzie ran to greet the sexy cop opening my front door.

"Your pizza is here," Steve announced with a takeout box in one hand and a white plastic bag in the other.

I followed him into the kitchen with my empty bowl. "Good, I'm starving."

"Looks like you just ate to me."

"That was this morning's breakfast that I never got around to eating. This," I said with a nod to the grease-stained box he had set on the counter, "is dinner."

Steve raised his hands in mock surrender while Fozzie inched closer, sniffing the air. "Far be it for me to get between a woman and her pizza."

"Wiser words have never been spoken." I pointed toward Fozzie's dog bed near the patio door. "That goes for dogs, too."

Fozzie turned and retreated to the table, no doubt waiting to scarf up the tasty bits of pepperoni that might fall his way.

Fat chance, dog.

"And I remembered your salad," Steve added, pulling a plastic bowl from the bag. "Or as we say at my house, your unnecessary filler."

"Salad is the correct terminology here. And thank you." I gave him a peck on the lips. "How'd it go at Eddie's?"

"Fine. It wasn't a league night, so the crowd was relatively light. Other than working the register and handing out bowling shoes while Eddie fixed the pinsetters, there wasn't a lot for me to do."

"Did you eat?" I asked, opening the pizza box to see the single remaining slice of his favorite meaty combo. "Never mind. I can see that you did."

He grinned. "I had to keep up my strength. You know,

after lifting all those bowling shoes. Besides, Rox insisted on feeding me."

As I knew she would.

After I reheated the pizza in the microwave, I carried my dinner to the kitchen table where Steve was waiting for me with a can of beer.

"Do you want some salad?" I asked him after heaping a small mountain of greens onto my plate. "I have plenty."

"There were onions and mushrooms on that pizza. I should've hit my veggie quota for the day."

"Says you."

Steve leaned back in his chair and leveled his gaze on me while Fozzie curled into a ball at his feet. "You can nag me about eating more vegetables after we get married."

I couldn't help but smile. "That will be my pleasure, but let's not call it nagging. Let's call it helping."

"You can call it anything you want." He pointed at my salad. "I'm still going to call that unnecessary filler."

"We'll work on varying your vocabulary after we get married, too."

Steve scoffed. "Good luck with that."

"Speaking of vocabulary words," I said, thinking that I might have stumbled upon a way to glean some information from him. "Karla had to write a report about how a motorcyclist hit a deer on Route 17 and then was found ten or fifteen feet down in some brush. It occurred to me as she was describing the scene that I wouldn't know what to call that."

"What to call what?"

"The word for that hillside. What did you call it in Kevin Lovely's accident report?"

"I didn't use one word. I just wrote what happened—that he veered off the road and careened twenty-five feet down a wooded slope until he hit that tree."

So far, so good. "Okay, so you basically described it like she did."

"That's what you want to do in a report—be accurate and descriptive." Narrowing his dark eyes, he seemed to be assessing me. "Which I'm sure you already know."

"Yes, but I want to use the right words and be as accurate as possible."

"Uh-huh."

"Of course, most of the time I'm talking to neighbors and family members—potential witnesses to what happened. And I put what they tell me in my report. But you do that too, right?"

Steve folded his arms, covering most of the Eddie's Place logo at the center of his black T-shirt. "Right."

"Like with that car accident, you talked to everyone who might have seen something, right?" I asked, watching him for a reaction.

He didn't move so much as an eyelash.

After ten seconds of staring at one another, he flashed me a satisfied smile. "Are you done?"

I stabbed a forkful of lettuce. "I don't know what you mean. I was just making conversation."

"Trying to pry information out of me is more like it."

"I wouldn't put it that way."

"I'm sure you wouldn't, but you really need to let this go."

"Thanks for the advice." But easier said than done.

Steve took a swig of beer, watching me while I ate.

"I get it, though," he said almost a minute later.

I looked up from the salad I no longer had an appetite for. "What?"

"It's natural for you to be curious. After all, it was Heather who dragged you into the middle of this on a couple of occasions."

That he knew of.

"And given the circumstances, I can see how she'd think that Lovely's death was suspicious. But, trust me." Steve rested his elbows on the table, effectively daring me to read his face. "There's nothing there. The guy died from his injuries after hitting that tree, plain and simple."

"And that's it? What about the time difference between the 911 calls?"

He shook his head. "Again, nothing there. So, can we please stop talking about this?"

That was also going to be easier said than done, because Steve had just lied to me.

Chapter Twenty-Five

People lie. For all sorts of reasons.

That was something that I had to come to understand at an early age.

What took longer was understanding the reasoning.

For that I needed some life experience to better understand human nature, to appreciate that a lie can be told with good intentions.

And that a lie told to me by someone close to me had to have a very good reason behind it because they would know that I'd recognize it as a lie.

I knew Steve as well as I knew anyone. Did I always understand his motives?

Heck, no. At least not at first.

But I loved and trusted him more than anyone I'd ever known, so I had no doubt that he had a very good reason for wanting me to believe that there was nothing significant about the gap of time between those 911 calls.

But I couldn't stop thinking about what that reason could be.

I was thinking about it when he left last night around

ten.

I was still thinking about it six hours later while listening to my dog snore.

And after I had warmed up my synapses with half a pot of coffee, a twenty-minute jog, and a long, hot shower, I came to the only conclusion that made any sense to me: There had to be another witness and he was trying to protect them.

That had to be why Steve dodged my question about finding out what the neighbors had seen or heard.

"So somebody else saw or heard the accident. So what?" I asked my reflection as I blasted my hair with my blow-dryer.

I sucked in a breath when an answer hit me. "What if their statement was radically different from Jonah's?"

It wouldn't be the first time that I'd heard about witnesses contradicting one another, but that could be a problem. Potentially for Jonah if he had lied about what he had seen.

Or lied for his mother.

Or his uncle Wyatt or whatever the heck Jonah called his father's cousin.

As Jonah told me that night out on his driveway, *"You don't know anything."* I didn't know much more now, but I intended to rectify that situation later this evening.

Since it was only five forty in the morning, much later. But that gave me plenty of time to flat-iron my hair, dive into my treasure trove of Glorious Organics freebies, and squeeze into the black wool suit I typically wore to funerals and court appearances.

Given the carton of mocha almond fudge I polished off after Steve left, I was both shocked and relieved that I could zip up my pants without some suck-it-all-in pantyhose.

Was this a sign that I was within a couple of pounds of fitting into my wedding dress?

Maybe.

I stared at the plastic garment bag that had been hanging in my closet for the last three months.

I could try it on and find out.

And do what if by some miracle I didn't look like an overstuffed cannoli?

I didn't have an answer to that question, but I knew I was going to need to come up with one soon.

If tonight went as I hoped it would and provided some answers about what really happened the night Kevin Lovely's car went off the road, maybe it was time.

Time to make some big decisions.

Really. Shouldn't I be ready to do that by now?

"Probably," I said to myself, wanting to commit to nothing beyond getting ready for tonight.

I had a more immediate need: jewelry. And I found just the piece.

Seconds later, I fastened the clasp of the pearl drop necklace Steve gave me last Christmas and then stepped around Fozzie for one last glimpse in the mirror.

Not bad for a mostly sleepless night.

I was as ready as I was going to get.

I was just twelve hours early. Plus, I had an hour to kill before the courthouse opened at seven.

Since it had been almost a week since I had checked in with Lucille and my great-aunt Alice, I gave Fozzie a goodbye hug and stepped through Duke's back door ten minutes later.

Alice glanced up from the dough she had been rolling out at her worktable. "You're here bright and early."

Bright? That wouldn't be happening anytime soon. Not with the thick dark clouds blanketing the area, making the full moon setting below them look like something out of a werewolf movie. The fog rising from the bay hovered over downtown, effectively casting a veil over all the streetlights.

"Have you looked outside?" I asked her. "There's nothing bright about it. Plus it's damp and creepy."

"Good point. Make that just early." Alice scanned me from head to toe as I stood in front of one of her industrial ovens to warm up. "You have your court duds on. What's going on? You sitting in on some big doings today?"

In a manner of speaking.

"I have a meeting later." I didn't want to mention with whom. The fewer people who knew that I'd be sitting down with two members of Kevin Lovely's family, the better.

Alice nodded, apparently satisfied. "If you're hungry, I've got some nice cream cheese scones that just came out of the oven."

Probably the one I had been standing in front of because the aroma venting from it had my mouth watering.

"Maybe later," I said, glancing at the golden beauties

tempting me from a cooling rack. My immediate task was to find Lucille and fuel myself with the latest gossip.

Duke arched an eyebrow as I approached. "You know you could go through the front door like everyone else who doesn't work here."

"I could, but what fun is that?" I kissed his grizzled cheek. "And good morning to you, too."

He nudged me away from the strips of bacon sputtering on his grill. "Git, or you're going to get to work smelling like grease."

Wouldn't be the first time, but that definitely wasn't the perfume I wanted to wear to this evening's meeting.

"I'm gonna get some coffee." And look for Lucille. "Want some?"

"Sure. Got a cup on the counter behind me."

I pushed open the swinging door and spotted Lucille taking an order at one of the booths along the back wall.

While I waited for her to make her way to the aluminum wheel over the grill, I headed toward the coffee station and said good morning to a man with matted graying hair sitting at the end of the counter.

His face was weathered and pale as the moon, his black eyes wide and alert, like a wild animal that had picked up the scent of danger.

When he didn't meet my gaze, instead focusing on the top button of my mulberry blouse as if it offered some safe haven, I wondered if he might be developmentally disabled. Then, he finally grunted something from behind his patchy beard and slid his empty cup and some body odor in my direction.

I grabbed a carafe and filled his cup. "Has someone taken your order?"

I got a nod and an unintelligible mumble before he took a loud slurp of coffee, again with no eye-contact.

He seemed to be content with Duke's crude-oil coffee, and I couldn't understand a word he said, so I returned to the kitchen with the carafe and a couple of cups.

"What'd that guy say to you?" Duke asked, watching me refill his coffee cup.

"Nothing much. At least nothing that I could make out."

"Lucille said that he seems a little off. Had a hard time getting his order."

By his rumpled flannel shirt and the stink clinging to him, I guessed he had been sleeping in the beater van I had seen parked near the front door. "I didn't sense any-thing to be concerned about. I think he's probably just used to keeping to himself." Probably for most of his adult life.

"If you say so," Duke muttered, stealing a glimpse of the guy while he plated a fluffy omelet, bacon, and toast. "Order up!"

"Don't worry about him. He's kind of stinky, but I'm pretty sure he's harmless." Unlike some people I had my doubts about.

"Two eggs over easy. Hash browns. Biscuit. And a short stack with bacon," Lucille called out as she tacked the order to the wheel.

Standing on my tiptoes to look over Duke's shoulder, I waved to get her attention.

Lucille brightened. "Hiya, kiddo."

I raised the carafe so that she could see it through the window. "When you have a second, come back and join Alice and me for a cup of coffee."

Lucille delivered the omelet order and popped back into the kitchen so quickly it was as if I'd put up the bat signal.

Duke pointed his spatula at her as she squeaked past. "You have exactly five minutes to finish that coffee."

She snorted. "Yeah, yeah."

"A little early for a break, isn't it?" Alice asked, watching me wipe two wooden stools free of the flour dust that covered every surface of her domain.

That was undeniable, and I knew Duke would chase me out of his kitchen with that spatula if this "break" went one minute over. "I'll make it fast. I just need some information."

My great-aunt's eyes widened. "What kind of information?"

"Yeah." Lucille eased herself onto the stool across from where I was sitting. "What's going on?"

I pushed one of the cups I had just filled toward her. "Nothing major. I need to get my loveseat recovered. Have you ever heard of McGowan & Son?" More specifically, Kevin Lovely's cousin?

Lucille frowned at me over the rim of her cup. "Dang! I thought you wanted to talk about something more interesting than furniture."

I did.

I turned to Alice. "Any scuttlebutt about the owner? I

hear he's sort of surly."

She shrugged. "Can't say I've ever met the man. What's the name again?"

"I think his name is Wyatt," I said. "Wyatt McGowan."

"Wyatt," Lucille repeated. "Seems to me I remember Candace down the street mentioning a Wyatt. A good-lookin' fella who fixed the banister in her house last year. That's not all she wanted him to do while he was there—if you catch my drift. So, if it's the same guy, I guess he's not *that* surly."

This wasn't the drift I had in mind. "Good to know."

"You might also be interested to know that he works with the Lovelys. They're the ones who did Candace's remodel. Now, I guess he just works with Veronica." Lucille's coral-painted lips pinched into a smirk. "But somethin' tells me you already knew that."

"I might have heard someone mention something about that," I admitted.

"Honey, are you asking about this guy because you suspect him of being involved in Kevin Lovely's death?" Alice asked.

"I'm just asking." I didn't dare say much more than that in front of the queen bee of Gossip Central. "I really do need to recover that loveseat and—"

"Get real," Lucille said. "You and I both know that wasn't *just* an accident."

Heck, we were now drifting into very dangerous territory. "No, I don't know that at all."

She pointed at me. "Well, you know somethin' or you

wouldn't be asking questions about this dude."

"I'm asking because my mother is considering doing some business with him." Which was partly true. "And it might not amount to anything, so—"

"But if he's someone who works with Veronica... Oh!" Alice drew in a sharp breath. "This has to do with that show idea of hers, doesn't it?"

Crap! I had forgotten that she and Duke had been there for Thanksgiving, when Marietta was blathering on about the Lovelys.

"What show idea?" Lucille asked.

"It's just an idea for a home improvement show that my mom got after she talked to the Lovelys about making over her kitchen." I shook my head. "I'm pretty sure it won't go anywhere, but it's still being discussed."

Lucille narrowed her eyes. "Interesting timing, don't you think?"

Yes, I did, but I sure didn't want to admit that to Duke's resident conspiracy theorist.

Instead, I shrugged. "I wouldn't make anything out of it."

"Well, you're here asking questions about this fella," Lucille said. "So you must—"

"Be looking out for my mother's best interests?" I smiled with enough sugar to put her into a diabetic coma. "Absolutely."

"Order up!" Duke barked.

Flattening her palms against the tabletop, Lucille pushed to her feet. "Sure, grin like the Cheshire cat. I'm not buying it. You think this guy had somethin' to do with Kevin Lovely takin' a header off that road."

"You're jumping to a really big conclusion," I said with a calm I didn't feel. "One that I wouldn't spread around because there is no basis behind it."

So please don't make this the gossip du jour.

Alice nodded. "I won't say a thing, not about the show either. Don't want to count chickens and all that."

Lucille grimaced. "I'm not so concerned about countin' chickens as I am about someone gettin' away with murder."

"Order up!" Duke bellowed in our direction. "As in right now!"

"We're not done here," Lucille said to me and then squeaked away.

But I was done and knew that I had better make myself scarce before she came back.

When I rose from the table, Alice glanced up from the pie crust she was fluting. "She means well. She just gets a little carried away sometimes. Especially with Miriam and some of the girls feeding her imagination with their theories about who done it."

Much like I'd had Heather feeding mine.

"Don't let her chase you away." Alice waved toward her husband's grill. "Have some breakfast. Better yet, if you wait a half hour, you could probably have it with Steve."

And give Lucille an open invitation to continue our conversation in front of the detective who investigated Kevin Lovely's accident? Not a chance!

"I need to get going, so I'll take a scone for later. And

maybe some bacon," I said with a wink.

Grabbing the carafe, I refilled Duke's cup on my way back to the coffee station. "Toss a couple of strips on the grill for me?"

He picked up the pack of bacon from the counter next to him. "You got it."

As I stepped through the swinging door, I noticed that the guy in the rumpled flannel shirt had his hand up like a schoolboy eager to answer the teacher's question.

"Something I can do for you?" I asked in my best customer service voice.

This time his eyes followed the carafe in my hand, and he pushed his cup toward me.

"A little more wake-up juice. Yes, sir." I filled his cup and then collected the plate that had been cleaned of every crumb. "It must have been good."

"G-good," he struggled to repeat, a hint of a smile forming below his soup-strainer mustache.

An actual word I could understand!

This felt like a tiny victory, and with the way my morning had been going, I was happy to take any win I could get.

"You have a good day," I said with the hope of coaxing more conversation out of him. "Be safe out there. It's really foggy, plus there's a full moon, so it's kind of creepy out."

He lifted his gaze back to my top button. "B-bad stuff happens when it's a f-full moon. *You* be safe out there."

Then he turned his focus to his coffee, signaling that he'd had enough conversation.

He wasn't the only one. Because I felt like I had just been warned.

Chapter Twenty-Six

I'm not a big believer in signs.

Sure, when my wedding planner mentioned that my ex and I shared the same destination wedding plans, I interpreted it as a sign.

A flashing red light type of stop sign.

If I didn't want to have another wedding in common with that man, I needed to change my plans.

Whether I chose to call it divine intervention, a reality check moment served on a silver platter by the universe, or dumb luck, I took it as seriously as a heart attack.

I didn't know how to take what the stinky guy at Duke's had said to me.

Do weird things happen when there's a full moon?

Yep.

In the hours before the moon set, Jan's car was side-swiped, a transformer blew, leaving the north end of town in the dark, and the Port Merritt Fire Department was called out after a cat knocked over some candles at one of those houses without electricity.

A logging truck also lost its load after swerving to

miss a herd of elk in the road out near Gibson Lake. But that happened closer to eight, so it's hard to blame the full moon for that bit of weirdness.

Still, I felt like today was a day in which I should proceed with caution.

It was definitely a don't walk under any ladders kind of day. A talk nicely to the antiquated copier day, even after it overheated and made an hour-long project take all flippin' morning. And since Patsy seemed to be hotter than the copier over a file that one of the junior prosecutors lost, it was a stay out of her sight day.

On my way to pick up Marietta after a quick trip home to feed Fozzie, the skies were just as dark and creepy as when I was talking to Mr. Stinky hours earlier. Only now, they rumbled with the thunderstorm that had moved in over the Olympic mountains.

The storm was miles away, but a restless wind was blowing, charging the cool air with a nervous energy.

No moon, no stars, hardly any oncoming headlights cutting through the darkness. Because everyone else must have had the good sense to stay home tonight.

The approaching storm only increased my sense of trepidation—something that my mother picked up on within seconds of infusing my car with her musky jasmine perfume.

"Good heavens, Charmaine. You're gripping that steering wheel like you're holding on for dear life."

"Am I?" I glanced down at my white knuckles. "It's been a weird day." And it wasn't over yet. Not by a long shot. "Lots of strange stuff going on, and now it looks like there's a thunderstorm headed our way. So I guess I'm just trying to be extra careful."

Marietta scoffed. "And people think I'm a nervous driver."

I decided to take the high road and not mention the crunched garage door we had driven away from moments earlier. "There's no harm in trying to be safe, especially on a night like this."

"Just don't go too slow," she said, fidgeting with the clutch bag on her lap as I turned left toward town. "I don't want to be late."

"We have plenty of time to get there. It's barely five forty-five." Had she been ready to go when I got to her door, she wouldn't have to worry about being late.

Since I wanted her cool, calm, and cooperative this evening, I kept that thought to myself.

"I just want to get there before they do," she said. "And run into the little girls' room beforehand. We wouldn't want nature to call at an inopportune moment."

With her walnut-sized bladder, those moments were practically guaranteed. But an inopportune moment for her could translate into an opportunity for me to talk to Veronica and Wyatt alone, so tonight that wasn't a bad thing.

After a couple of minutes of silence in which the only sound was my phone dinging with a text message, my mother leaned toward me to smooth a lock of my hair.

"Is something wrong?" I asked, taking a swipe at my overly long bangs before she did.

"Not at all." She settled back in her seat. "You look very nice. Thanks for making the effort."

Which none too subtly implied that she didn't approve of how I usually dressed. "No problem."

My phone dinged again.

"Do you want me to see what that's about?" Marietta asked.

"No." I was sure it was from Crystal. "That's okay. I'll check it out later." Much later, when my mother wasn't around.

Marietta flipped down the mirrored visor and spent the rest of the drive primping while complaining every time I hit a tiny pothole.

"Charmaine, stop it," she huffed with her lipstick wand in hand when we made impact with pothole number four.

"It's the road! I'm not doing anything beyond trying to get us there." Which couldn't happen soon enough.

"Well, try harder."

"I'm doing my best." To maintain my cool.

But you have got to chill out, I wanted to yell at her. Instead, I wrapped my hands so tightly around the steering wheel the horn honked.

"What was that?" Marietta asked, flipping the visor up with a snap.

"Nothing. Everything's fine." I pointed at the illuminated sign for the Bayside up ahead. "We're almost there and with time to spare."

"What a relief."

She could say that again.

Marietta flipped the mirrored visor down and gave her choppy cropped hair one last fluff before snapping it back up. "I have to admit that I'm a little nervous."

And her nervousness wasn't helping mine.

"At least I appear to know what I'm doing, right?" she asked as I slowed behind another car turning into the parking lot of the Bayside. "Which, of course, I can fake as long as I look presentable. So, what do you think?"

Presentable! Was she kidding?

Wearing a forest green belted jacket with a matching slit skirt that showed off her legs and emerald teardrop earrings, my mother looked more than presentable. She was camera-ready perfection. "You look terrific."

Marietta beamed. "I really want this to go well."

So did I. "It's going okay so far, 'cause we're five minutes early."

"Great, that should give me enough time to make a quick trip to the ladies' room."

As my headlights illuminated the interior of the black Jeep Wrangler in front of us, I recognized the man be-hind the wheel. A woman with shoulder-length hair sat in the passenger seat. "Okay, but I'm pretty sure that's Veronica in that Jeep."

"Shoot! I wanted to be sitting at our table to receive them."

"Then we should have left earlier."

I immediately bit my tongue. Now wasn't the time to get pissy, especially if I wanted to keep my seat at that table.

Marietta groaned low in her throat, sounding like a

lioness that wouldn't hesitate to bite more than my tongue if another smart remark escaped from my lips. "Just park the car."

We were barely in the lot. "Give me a second."

"Park the car now!" my mother demanded when Wyatt took the first available spot.

I pulled into the next open space, three cars down from the Wrangler, and before I had shut off the ignition, Marietta had one foot out the door.

"Hello!" she called out, skittering toward Wyatt McGowan and Veronica as fast as her four-inch heels would carry her.

If I wanted to keep up, I didn't have time to put on my hooded coat, so I fetched it from the backseat and ran toward the awning-covered entrance of the Bayside.

The wind whipping my hair into my face had acted like a mute button for all the conversation that had taken place in the parking lot. But it seemed like it had been pleasant enough, and judging by my mother's buoyant face as she herded them inside, her mood had mercifully improved.

Following the women into the restaurant, I finger-combed my hair back and smiled at the man holding open the door. "Hi. Nice to see you again."

Wyatt nodded, dressed in a black leather jacket over charcoal slacks and looking as somber as a funeral director. "Nice to see you, too."

No, it wasn't.

He might be someone who needed a little time to warm up to strangers, as Crystal had suggested, but the muscle twitching at his jaw told me he didn't want to have anything to do with me.

Tough. You're stuck with me for the next hour.

"I'm Charmaine," I said, extending my hand to him. "Marietta's daughter."

He shook my hand like an automaton. "Wyatt McGowan."

"I take it you already met my mother." Because I had seen them shake hands in the parking lot.

"We met," he answered, not bothering to mask his level of underwhelm.

Okay, so much for the niceties.

"Our table's ready," my mother gleefully announced as if we were setting off on an adventure.

And maybe we were.

It was a kind of exploration after all.

For Marietta and Veronica, a next step toward reality show fame and fortune.

For me, a step closer toward finding out what really happened the day that Kevin Lovely died.

As for Wyatt, he begrudgingly followed Veronica while scanning his surroundings as if the hostess was leading us into danger.

If Veronica had provided him any information about why we were here, it couldn't have been much because Wyatt looked as wary as Mr. Stinky when we reached our corner table in the mostly deserted restaurant.

"There, isn't this nicer than that crowded, noisy bar?" Marietta said once the hostess was out of earshot.

Wyatt frowned at Veronica sitting next to him. "What

is this?"

She winked across the table at my mother before aiming a sweet-as-sugar smile at him. "I told you. It's an opportunity—a tremendous opportunity that Ms. Moreau here is being kind enough to talk to us about."

If Veronica had intended for that to impress him, she had misjudged the big guy.

He stared bullets back at her. "An opportunity," he repeated as if they were dirty words.

She stared right back at him. "All I ask is that you keep an open mind."

Wyatt looked over his shoulder for our waitress. "I think I'm gonna need that drink."

Over the next ten minutes, while Marietta outlined her vision for the show, referencing several popular home improvement shows that she'd probably never heard of prior to last week, I sat next to her and watched the dynamics between Veronica and Wyatt.

Most notable was the lack of engagement.

With the space between them, they could have been strangers on a bus.

They didn't touch. Not once.

In the few times they had exchanged glances, there had been no spark of sexual energy. No heat between them whatsoever.

In fact, there was surprisingly little warmth.

Clearly, they possessed a comfort with one another, which was natural considering their family connection. But I saw nothing to suggest that these two had ever been lovers. Or in that moment, had a relationship that could survive this meeting because Wyatt looked like a volcano that was seconds away from erupting.

His brows were an uncompromising slash as he glowered at Veronica. "You can't be serious."

"Think about it," she told him. "This is a chance for us to really grow our businesses. This could put us both on the map!"

Wyatt vented a breath. "I don't need to grow my business. I'm already so busy that I can barely keep up with it."

"With the show as another revenue stream, you could easily afford to hire some help," Marietta chimed in.

The muscle in his jaw ticked down to his impending eruption. "Good craftsmanship doesn't grow on trees."

"Exactly," she said, quick to agree. "And when it's blended with interesting personalities and wrapped in a package that will appeal to the ladies in our audience... Well, that's something I can sell to the network."

Marietta lowered her voice as if she were sharing a secret. "That's the *it* factor. And as a couple, you've got it in spades."

"We're not a couple," he stated matter-of-factly.

True. No wonder I hadn't detected any heat between them.

Wyatt scowled at Veronica, generating plenty of heat of his own. "So, can we stop—"

"Hear her out, please," she said with a nod to my mother to continue.

"When I say 'couple,' I mean that's how the public would perceive you, as on-screen partners." Marietta flicked her wrist as if the word choice were unimportant. "What matters is the relationship, both familial and as business associates, your banter as you tackle projects together. Really, it could be fun for you as well as the audience."

The lips of the big man sitting across from me curled into a taut, humorless smile. "Fun."

Tick, tick, tick.

Wyatt chugged the last of his scotch. "Nothing about this would be fun. This would be crazy, and I've heard more than enough."

"Oh, no, you haven't," Veronica countered, sounding like a mother accustomed to dealing with willful children. "We're going to talk this out. We have to seriously consider this, because things are different now. I have kids to put through college, and with Kevin gone... I need to do what's best for them."

She placed her palm on his thick forearm, touching him for the first time this evening as she blinked away tears. "I know this has come as a surprise, but will you at least consider what this venture could mean for Kevin's children?"

Wyatt grumbled an obscenity, but he didn't make any move to leave.

Surprisingly, the only one to do that was sitting next to me.

"Why don't we give the two of you a few minutes of privacy," Marietta said, scooting back in her seat and tapping my thigh to signal that I should do the same.

What? Leave the second Kevin's name got dropped?

This business meeting of hers had just started to get interesting!

My mother cocked her head, giving me the parental move it or lose it look.

Fine!

Smiling dutifully, I pushed back my chair and grabbed my tote bag. "Excuse us."

She then hooked my arm as we made our way toward the lobby, Marietta's celebrity status turning a few heads in the process. "He's not making this easy, but if anyone can win that man over, I'm confident Veronica can."

"Maybe." Veronica had certainly known what to say to keep Wyatt's butt planted in that seat. What to do, too. Play the "we need to do this for Kevin's children" card.

Stepping aside for a couple exiting the bar, Marietta shot me a sideways glance. "I realize that I can't *read* people the way you can, but she strikes me as the kind of woman who can be very persuasive."

"I'm sure you're right." Because Crystal Zimmerman had said as much when I met with her Sunday.

"I hope so, because the show won't get picked up unless we have someone like him." My mother took a step toward the hallway that divided the dining area from the bar. "Where's the restroom? They need a sign."

There was a sign. She was just too distracted to read it. Plus, she wasn't wearing her glasses. "End of the hall on the right."

Marietta looked back at me "Aren't you coming?"

"I don't need to go." And I wanted to stand where I

could see our table in case the discussion there got heated.

Grimacing at my hair, she crooked a finger for me to follow her. "Trust me, you do."

Great.

I followed her into the ladies' room and sighed when I saw my wind-swept reflection in the mirror. "I swear I don't know why I bother flat-ironing my hair. It's just going to do what it wants, especially in this weather."

"My darling, what you need is a good haircut," Marietta said over the flush of the toilet in the next stall.

"I need more than that." I needed to contain my unruly mop with the tortoiseshell clip that should have been in the side pocket of my tote.

"I thought I recognized that voice," Crystal said, pumping the soap dispenser at the sink next to me.

Yikes! A stall door was the only thing separating Crystal and my mother.

Praying that door would remain closed, I abandoned the search for my hairclip and pasted a smile on my face. "Hey, fancy meeting you here."

"I know," Crystal said. "Small world, huh?"

Way too small.

"And I hear you," she added, drying her hands. "This wind makes it hard to have a good hair day."

My hair was now the least of my concerns.

"Yours looks great. I give up on mine." I slung my tote over my shoulder as if I were ready to leave, hoping she'd follow my lead.

Despite having her coat and purse in hand, she made

no move toward the door. Instead, Crystal's gaze slanted to the occupied stall and she lowered her voice. "That wouldn't be your mother in there, would it?"

Crap, crap, crap!

How could I answer that question so that this real estate agent wouldn't wait expectantly for an introduction to her fake client?

"Yes, and she has a shy bladder," I whispered. "So let's give her a little privacy."

Crystal nodded, but not without some obvious disappointment. "No problem. I just thought—"

"I know." Oh, boy, did I know, since I was the one who had dangled a fat commission in front of her like a shiny fishing lure.

It was only natural that Crystal should want to bite, but that couldn't happen. Not tonight of all nights, and certainly not in a bathroom!

I needed to keep these two women separate like the streams in *Ghostbusters*, because it would be very, very bad if they should cross paths.

Specifically for me.

"I'll wait for you outside," I told my mother.

"Okay, I'll be out in a minute," she said.

I knew she hadn't factored in the time she'd spend primping in front of the mirror and figured that I had a maximum of five minutes to get rid of Crystal.

Since she was holding her coat, I could only hope that Crystal had been making a pit stop prior to heading home. "Sorry, for a public person my mother requires an inordinate amount of privacy sometimes."

She pressed her lips together as if she were having trouble swallowing the pack of lies I had been telling. "Is that all this is?" she asked over the din of the crowded bar behind us. "Or is something wrong?"

Something was very wrong. But it wasn't the "bad stuff" Mr. Stinky had warned me about. This debacle was of my own making.

"Not at all." I pointed to the exit. "Let's step outside where it's quieter." And where no one from my table could see us.

"Actually, I was leaving anyway."

"Great!" I mentally kicked myself for sounding too happy about that. "I'll walk you to your car."

Putting on her coat, Crystal led the way toward the Cadillac I had seen parked in her driveway. "You've barely replied to any of my texts. You're sure nothing's wrong?"

"Sorry, I've just been busy," I said, hugging my arms to my chest as wind gusts blasted my backside. "And my mother's time has been consumed on a project she has in the works." At least that much was true. "But I hope she'll have some time to review all the information you've sent us by the end of the week."

Because I couldn't continue on with this charade.

What did I even have to show for it?

Nothing.

I was no closer to understanding what happened the night of Kevin Lovely's accident than I was a week ago.

After Crystal and I said our goodbyes, I stood alone in the parking lot and thought about Kevin's widow sitting inside the Bayside. If anyone knew what happened that night, she would.

But what was I supposed to do? Go in there and ask why she didn't call 911 right away? Imply that my mother's would-be reality show star had caused her husband's death?

That would go over like a lead balloon, one that would forever sink Marietta's chances of taking her dream show to a network.

No. I wouldn't find any answers sitting at that table, but as long as Veronica Lovely remained there with my mother, it could be the perfect time to go out and look for some.

A flash of lightning backlit the inky clouds, followed by a clap of thunder, and once again, I felt like I was being warned to proceed with caution.

Chapter Twenty-Seven

My mother wasn't happy with me when I told her that I wasn't feeling well.

Wyatt McGowan was even more unhappy with me when Veronica offered to drive Marietta home, just as I had hoped.

Since the three of them had ordered another round of drinks, I figured I had a minimum of an hour before the headlights of Wyatt's Jeep might sweep over a parked Subaru that didn't belong in Veronica Lovely's neighborhood.

To my advantage, there were no streetlights to illuminate the winding lane that led to her house. And of the three houses at the foot of the hill where Kevin had crashed into that tree, only two of them had their porch lights on.

It was a little after seven on this now-rainy evening, so the odds should have been good that someone would be home to answer the door. Whether anyone had been around at the time of the accident was another matter entirely, but I would never have a better opportunity to see what I could find out.

Using the flashlight on my phone, I went to the door of the split-level house across the street from the crash site. No lights were on outside or inside, and the spider webs clinging to the corners of the covered porch gave the place an eerie haunted house feel.

After ringing the doorbell and hearing nothing but raindrops pattering on the roof, I hurried next door to a mocha-brown rambler with several lights on. Before I climbed the steps to the front door, I heard a chorus of yappy dogs sounding the intruder alert.

I retrieved my notebook, a pen, and my deputy coroner badge from my tote, rang the doorbell, and listened to another minute of barking. Finally, a heavy-set, bald man with glasses appeared in the doorway.

I didn't recognize him, and he looked at me as if he had no interest in buying whatever I was selling.

That meant that he also didn't recognize me.

Good. I didn't want my visit to her neighborhood to get back to Veronica.

"Hi," I said, showing him my badge just long enough to appear official. "I'm following up on the accident that took place across the street a week ago Friday."

He pushed his glasses up the bridge of his thick nose while his dogs continued to yap from another room of the house. "Yeah?"

"Were you home at the time of the accident, Mr. ...?" I asked, hoping he'd provide me his name.

"Leggett. Mike Leggett. Don't get home until close to six most nights. I saw the ambulance arrive, though."

"Anyone else home before that? Maybe around four-thirty?"

He shook his head. "My wife was at her mother's up in Port Angeles. Big Thanksgiving weekend reunion that I didn't stay for."

"Okay. After you got home, did you talk to anyone who might have seen or heard the accident?"

"I talked to a couple of the neighbors who came out to see what was going on. Inez seemed to be the only one who heard anything," he said, pointing to the house around the bend from where Kevin Lovely's car went off the road.

While thunder rumbled in the distance, I thanked him and took the short trek in the steady rain to a white stucco house with asparagus green shutters. My heart skipped a beat when I saw the name "Avila" on the mailbox because I knew Inez Avila as one of the seniors who frequently stopped by Duke's Cafe for pancakes after her morning exercise class.

She not only knew me, she also knew Gram, Steve, and most of the people I worked with. That meant I had to be very, very careful with what questions I asked, because I couldn't afford to give Mrs. Avila the impression that I was poking around in any official capacity.

In other words, I was going to have to come up with some creative lie. Again.

Standing under the roof of the front porch, I pushed back the hood of my raincoat and rang the doorbell.

I could see the flicker of a TV through a crack in her front curtain, but no one came to the door.

Instead, Mrs. Avila pulled back that curtain and peered out.

I waved and her guarded expression immediately changed to one of recognition. Seconds later, the arched front door swung open to something that sounded like a Spanish language soap opera on in the background of her living room.

Standing in socks and wearing baggy sweatpants and a fuzzy peach sweater, Inez Avila looked shorter and wider than I remembered. I also didn't remember the aluminum walker she was gripping.

"Charmaine," Mrs. Avila said, giving me a warm smile. "What brings you here on a night like this?"

"It's something I hope you can help me with. Do you have a few minutes?"

"Of course." She shuffled back with the walker. "Come in."

"Sorry I'm so wet," I said, shaking off my coat before I stepped onto her slate entryway.

"Not to worry. There's nothing sacred in here other than my Chica," she said with a soft lilt to her accent as she beamed at the marmalade cat curled into a ball on a nubby striped loveseat.

After clicking off her flat screen, Mrs. Avila slowly pushed her walker toward a compact kitchen that smelled of cumin and onions, and whatever else that remained in the pot on her stove. "May I offer you anything? Maybe some tea to warm you up?"

"Only if you're going to have some."

"I was just about to make some. Helps me sleep, and

at my age, I can use all the help I can get."

I had no idea how old this diminutive lady was. Her hair swept back in a braided bun was streaked with silver, but few age lines marred her olive complexion. I remembered Lucille telling me how Inez and her parents had fled from Cuba to escape the revolution, so I guessed she was close to seventy.

I followed her into the kitchen, where colorful crayon artwork covered the front of an old, white refrigerator. "Have a seat," she said with a nod toward a rectangular oak table surrounded by four straight-back chairs. "Is hibiscus tea okay?"

I was no tea connoisseur. More than anything, I wanted the time it would afford me. "That's fine," I said, draping my coat over the back of the closest chair.

Noticing her moving very gingerly as she angled the walker in front of a cupboard, I set down my tote and came to her side. "Can I help?"

Mrs. Avila aimed a plump index finger at the bottom shelf. "If you could hand me that red box."

"No problem," I said, placing it by the stove so that she could keep both hands on the walker. "Anything else I can do?"

"The cups are up there."

I followed her gaze and took two ceramic mugs from the cupboard by the sink.

She heaved a sigh when I set them down on her gold-speckled Formica counter and picked up the tea kettle to fill it with water.

"Some hostess I am," she lamented, favoring one leg

as she stood by the stove. "You're doing all the work."

Leaning back against the counter, I gave her what I hoped was a reassuring smile. "I think it's a little easier for me."

"I have to admit that nothing is easy for me right now." Mrs. Avila dragged her walker closer to the stove to turn on the burner under the tea kettle. "But at least I am moving better with this thing now."

"What happened, if you don't mind me asking."

"Hip replacement. Two weeks ago." She clucked her tongue. "Horrible timing to schedule it right before a holiday, but that was when my daughter—she is a teacher—could stay with me after I got out of the hospital."

For how long? Long enough to be another potential witness? "Then she was here when that accident happened up around the bend?"

"No. She left earlier that day." Mrs. Avila's dark brown eyes narrowed. "Is that why you are here? To ask about that accident?"

"Actually, yes. I work for the county and some paperwork got misfiled," I said hanging my head in shame to sell the yarn I was spinning. "So—"

"You work for Frankie. Is that not what I heard from Lucille a year or two ago?"

This was the major downside of small-town life. Almost everyone knew everything worth knowing about everyone else's friends and neighbors.

I nodded. "It's embarrassing to admit that this is probably my fault, but if I could find out who all gave a statement that day to Ben Santiago, I might be able to find the file."

"Oh," she said over the hiss of the water coming to a boil. "I got you, but you are here awfully late to be asking about paperwork."

Mrs. Avila got me, all right. Right in the middle of a big, fat lie and the only thing I could think to do was to keep plumping it up. "I need to find it before some people I work with discover that it's missing."

"I see." She turned off the burner. "Well, I think it is going to be a pretty short list of the folks around here who provided a statement."

I watched her pour steaming water over the teabags in the mugs. "Does that include you?"

"As far as I know, it is only me. And some family members, of course." She shuffled a couple of steps back with the walker. "Charmaine, would you mind carrying these into the living room? I am most comfortable where I can stretch out my leg."

"Go ahead. I'll bring your tea to you once you're settled."

I used those few seconds to grab my pen and notebook, and then I joined Mrs. Avila with the steaming mugs. "You were saying that your daughter had left before the time of the accident."

Mrs. Avila winced as she lowered herself into one of the two recliners facing the flat screen mounted on the wall.

"Are you okay?" I asked, handing her one of the mugs.

She sucked in a deep breath, a flush in her cheeks

from the exertion. "I'm fine. Getting up and down … still not so easy."

I took a seat on the matching chocolate brown recliner to her left. It had an indentation in the seat, probably from the girth of her late husband. While I waited for Mrs. Avila to take a sip of tea and relax, I placed my notebook on my lap and tried to do the same.

"I'm sorry," she said. "You asked something about my daughter?"

"Yes. You mentioned that she left earlier in the day." I wanted her to pick up the story from there.

"Around two. It was my granddaughter's birthday and a bunch of nine-year-olds were coming over for a slumber party, so Maya had better things to do than hang out here with me all day."

"Okay, then you were here by yourself around four-thirty. In case we need to reconstruct your statement."

Like I would have the authority to do such a thing, but I had to say something to keep her talking.

Much to my relief, she nodded. "Yes. Just me and Chica."

"And that's when you heard the car crash?" I asked, feeling like I was finally on the verge of understanding what happened that day.

"Oh, no. I had taken a pain pill an hour earlier and was sound asleep."

What?!

Chapter Twenty-Eight

Mrs. Avila swallowed a sip of tea. "I am usually not such a sound sleeper, especially during the day, but those pills really knock me out."

I was confused. "But you said that you provided a witness statement to Ben Santiago."

"And Steve," she said, smiling at me like a proud mother. "Your fiancé was very nice and polite. You should have seen how he took charge of the situation."

I wished I had.

"The way he climbed up and down that hill, measuring everything, taking pictures." Mrs. Avila nodded with approval. "Very good at his job, I think."

"I think so, too." But I didn't want to talk about what she saw Steve doing because that would have been well after Kevin Lovely's car hit that tree.

I wanted her to back up to what caused her to get out of bed. "So, you didn't hear anything at the time of the accident? That wasn't what woke you up?"

"It's like I told Steve," Mrs. Avila said, resting her mug on the arm of her recliner. "I thought I was dreaming at first. I also had the TV on in the bedroom. An old Burt Reynolds movie that I had fallen asleep in the middle of. I always liked his movies. Anyway, I was not sure what I heard. It sounded like a bang, but it was all the barking that made me think that something was wrong."

"Barking." I looked up from the notes I had been scribbling. "Somebody's dog was barking?"

"Barking something terrible."

"What time was this?" I asked.

"I am not sure exactly. I told Steve and Ben that it was probably around four-thirty, but that was only because it was almost dark by the time I got outside to see what was going on." Annoyance tugged at the corners of Mrs. Avila's mouth. "It took me a while because Maya was not here to help me put on my shoes. I still cannot manage that. Just hurts too much to bend over. Eventually, I was able to slip on the big, rubber boots I use for gardening, but that took forever."

I estimated "forever" to be at least ten minutes. "Okay, so it might have been close to four forty-five by the time you got your coat on and headed outside."

She shrugged. "Maybe around then. That's when I saw the boy's dog—a Great Dane—running through my yard."

"What boy?"

"Veronica's boy. Nice boy. He always walks the dog in the afternoon."

"Jonah," I said.

"Right. Jonah. I did not see him anywhere. Not at first, but his dog was running around, dragging his leash on the ground and barking like crazy, so that made me think something had happened to the boy."

With tears pooling in her dark eyes, Mrs. Avila met my gaze. "Then, when I started following the dog up the hill, I heard him. The boy—Jonah—calling for help down by the car. I thought at first that he had been a passenger in the car and asked him if he was hurt, but he said he was okay. That he had jumped from one of the big rocks down there to help his father but could not get back up. That it was his father that needed help."

This wasn't what I had expected to hear.

"It was just you out there with him? No cars went by?" Like a Jeep Wrangler. "No other neighbors came out of their houses to see what was going on?"

Mrs. Avila shook her head. "Not too many of us live down here. Too steep. Floods every couple of years. That is why it is just the Leggetts and me right now. Myrna Swenson lives next door to the Leggetts, but she always goes to Arizona this time of year. So, it was just me, since Mr. Leggett does not get home that early. No cars. No nobody. And three days after surgery, I was moving very slowly with my walker."

She still was.

"It was one of those moments I wish I had a cell phone. I just never thought I needed one," she added, wiping away a tear. "But I could have called 911. Jonah begged me to call for help because he could not get inside the car to his father's phone. The door would not open and his father was too hurt to move. I thought about going back to my house to make the call, but I was already halfway up the hill and with the boy crying for his mother, I just tried to get to her as quickly as I could."

Holy smokes! "You must have walked half a mile." Most of it uphill. That was a lot for anyone who had just gotten out of the hospital.

Mrs. Avila shrugged. "It had to be done. There was no one else. When I rounded the bend up there, I saw Veronica in her yard, calling for Jonah. I waved at her and she started running. I told her there had been an accident and for her to call for the ambulance. Then I hurt so bad I just stood at the end of the cul-de-sac and waited for someone to drive me back down the hill." She chuckled humorlessly. "There was no way I could walk back. They would need to call for an ambulance for me if I tried."

As if Chica had sensed that Mrs. Avila needed a little comfort after reliving her ordeal, the cat jumped up onto the arm of the recliner and sweetly rubbed her head against the woman's shoulder.

"That was not a good day for any of us, was it, Chica?" Mrs. Avila said, running her hand over the cat's ear. Then she turned back to me. "And that is pretty much everything that I told Steve and Ben that night. In case you need to recreate the statement, it is enough, yes?"

"Absolutely that's enough." Because the puzzle pieces surrounding Kevin Lovely's death had just clicked into place.

Every piece but one, which I didn't know if Inez Avila could supply.

"This won't be included in your statement," I said. "But I'm curious. How did the accident even happen? Did you ever find out?"

"I do not know all the details, but I was there with Veronica when one of the firemen helped Jonah up the hill." Pulling a tissue from the box on the table between us, Mrs. Avila dabbed at the fresh tears spilling over her lashes. "The poor boy just cried and cried, and said he was sorry as his mama held him in her arms. That he didn't mean for the accident to happen."

"But it couldn't have been his fault. He's just a kid."

Inez Avila nodded with one of the saddest smiles I had ever seen. "He stepped in front of the car, and I guess the dog got spooked and maybe that was when his father had to swerve to miss him? I am not sure. I heard Jonah say something about an argument, and that he was just trying to stop his father from leaving."

I thought about what Jonah had told me out on his driveway—that I didn't know what he had been going through since his dad's death. Now I understood what he meant.

He blamed himself.

"He is a good boy," Mrs. Avila insisted, jabbing a finger toward my notebook as if she wanted me to quote her. "This was not his fault."

I prayed that Jonah would get some help so that he could believe that as well.

After thanking Mrs. Avila for her time, I returned my mug to the kitchen and gathered my things.

"Good luck finding that file," she said with a wave

from her recliner as I headed for the door.

I should have felt awful for making up that story to get this nice lady to talk to me, but I didn't. I gave her another thank-you, feeling a tremendous sense of relief as I stepped off her porch and into the pouring rain.

The gnawing at my gut that Kevin Lovely had been a victim of foul play now just felt like hunger pangs.

Probably because I had missed dinner.

I was sorely tempted to get in my car and head straight to Duke's for a patty melt and a large order of fries, but I needed to make a stop on the way.

Chapter Twenty-Nine

"So, it really was just an accident?" Heather asked, huddled on her sofa with her knees drawn to her chest. "You're sure she wasn't involved?"

I nodded and inched away from the wood stove that was making my damp slacks feel like I had been cooking them in a rice steamer. "Veronica called 911 as soon as her neighbor told her what had happened. Really, given how badly Kevin was hurt, it might not have made any difference if she'd been able to call sooner."

Heather's eyes narrowed. "Well, we'll never know that, will we."

I couldn't disagree, although I didn't think I deserved the snippy tone. "We'll never know."

Staring down at the Irish setter laying between us on the hardwood floor, Heather muttered an expletive.

I thought that might be her last word on the subject, which was perfectly okay with me. I had nothing else to say. Plus, the kitchen would be closing in twenty minutes, so if I wanted that patty melt, I needed to hit the road.

Then, Heather released a low, bitter chuckle while shaking her head. "And all this because Kevin swerved to miss a *dog*."

I left out the part about Jonah standing in the middle of the road with that dog. "That's what I was told."

"Incredible," she said with another shake of her head. "Just effing incredible."

I didn't have anything to say to that either.

After a beat of silence, Heather scrubbed her face as if she wanted to wash away all the hurt of the last twelve days. "So, that's that."

"That's that." I studied the woman who used to be my best friend. With her toffee-blond hair spilling over the shoulders of her flannel pajama top and her glowing pink cheeks, she looked so much like my old grade school buddy, it made my heart ache. "You okay?"

She slowly nodded. "I will be."

"Okay, then," I said, making my way to the rack in her entryway, where I had hung my drippy raincoat and tote. "Let me know if—"

"You're not leaving already, are you?"

I guess not.

"I can stay for a few more minutes." I glanced up the stairs at the sound of her son playing a video game in his room. "Maybe until you need to get Robby to bed."

Pushing up from the sofa, Heather waved me off. "He's ten. He gets himself to bed. Want some wine?"

The only thing I wanted to hit my gullet was some greasy fast food, but this didn't seem like the time for total honesty. "Sure."

She crossed the room with Ginger following close behind and stopped at the foot of the stairs. "Fifteen minutes 'til bedtime," she called up. "Be sure to brush your teeth."

"Okay," Robby dutifully responded.

"He'll stretch that into thirty. He's like me. He likes to read himself to sleep, so I'll have to pry that book out of his hands in a half hour," Heather said, leading me and Ginger past a dining room and into a gorgeous, updated kitchen with a center island. "In the meantime, white or red?"

"White, please." Standing in the doorway, I took a mental inventory of her top-of-the-line appliances and the Italian marble countertops gleaming under a half-dozen recessed lights in the ceiling. New cabinets with glass panel doors displayed her set of blue and white dishes, complementing the similar cheerful pattern in her floor tile.

"What do you think?" Heather asked when our gazes met.

"It's beautiful." I had never been inside her house before and had no idea what her kitchen used to look like, but whoever had transformed this space had a keen eye for design as well as functionality.

Given her history with Kevin Lovely, I assumed it had been his wife.

I also assumed that Heather must have taken out a second mortgage to pay for it.

She beamed with pride. "Kevin finished it on my birthday."

Which was July tenth, two weeks after mine. I re-membered because we used to celebrate them together.

"I never thought I'd be able to afford Italian marble," she said, her eyes glistening like twin oceans, her voice thick with emotion. "But Kevin gave me a discount. He said it was a birthday present."

Of course he did.

"That was good of him." What else could I say? Ask what she gave him in exchange?

She cleared her throat. "Anyway, I figured that I'd be living here until Robby leaves home so I might as well make it as nice for us as possible. The upstairs bathroom was going to be next, but…"

But Kevin's widow might not be as eager to offer a discount to his lover?

Heather removed two blue-stemmed wineglasses from the cupboard next to the sink. "Some new wallpa-per might be all I can afford for a while."

I had no encouraging words to offer in response, no witty remarks to lighten the mood. Heck, after twenty-five years of barely speaking to one another, I didn't know how to carry on a normal conversation with her.

While Heather worked the corkscrew, I occupied my-self by studying the framed photos hanging outside her kitchen doorway. One with mother and son hamming it up in matching Harry Potter costumes was cute. The recent one next to it with Robby proudly holding a huge salmon was even cuter.

"He looks like you," I told Heather when she handed me a glass.

"You think so?" Focusing on the picture of her son, she sighed. "Half the time all I can see is his dad in him."

"Then you're not seeing things objectively, 'cause Robby looks so much like you did at that age, it's incredible."

"I guess," she conceded, staring into the blue eyes that matched hers.

"He seems like a great kid."

"He's a good boy. Much sweeter than I deserve." She padded across the hardwood in thick socks with Ginger's toenails clicking as she followed.

"Well, you've now seen the new kitchen," Heather said, taking one end of the sofa while I sat at the other end. "And you know everything there is to know about what's been going on with me. Tell me about you."

Swallowing a sip of chardonnay, I couldn't help but wonder why she wanted me to stay.

Was it that she simply didn't want to be alone and wanted some girl talk to take her mind off Kevin?

It certainly seemed that way. But with me? I should be the last female in her life that Heather would want to chat up.

Okay, second to last after Veronica.

"You already know what I've been up to lately," I said.

Her mouth tightened with a pucker. "Other than that."

Since talking about Steve was a no-go, I went with the first safe subject that popped into my head. "You know, the usual. Work has been keeping me pretty busy, and now with the holidays—"

"Yeah, yeah. Tell me what's going on with your wedding."

I could feel my cheeks flush, and I knew it wasn't from two sips of wine. "My wedding?"

"What?" She stared at me over her wineglass. "Is that a sore subject?"

"No. Of course not," I lied for the umpteenth time tonight.

"Good. Because I want to hear about something good for a change."

But I didn't know what to say, so I took another drink.

Settling back against a pillow, Heather tucked one leg under her. "So? When's the big day?"

I averted my gaze to the engagement ring sparkling on my finger. "I don't know."

"You don't know?" She snorted. "You, who always had to plan our birthday parties down to the last little detail, don't know?"

I glared at her for throwing what should have been a happy memory for both of us into my face. "Excuse me if I don't find that funny."

"Okay, I'm sorry if somebody's having cold feet."

"I'm *not* having cold feet. The wedding's just on pause for a little while."

"Because...?"

I blew out a breath of exasperation. "I don't know. I guess I'm just waiting for things to settle down so that I can really think about what to do."

"What's there to think about?" she said, her volume

rising. "Either the two of you want to get married or you don't."

"It's a bit more complicated than that."

"Only if you make it complicated."

I frowned at her. "I don't think you understand. I have to find a venue, find someone to marry us, it has to be a time when Steve can get off work—"

Making a face, Heather dismissively waved her hand as if I had held a wedge of limburger cheese under her nose. "Or you fly off to Vegas on a Friday, get married by an Elvis impersonator, and you're back to work Monday morning."

I couldn't help but smirk. "An Elvis impersonator?"

She shrugged. "Hey, if you're gonna have a Vegas wedding, do it right."

"I don't want a Vegas wedding."

"Then go to Hawaii if you want a destination wedding. Isn't that what you had originally planned?"

I was surprised Heather knew about that. "My ex got married there. Had the same wedding planner and everything. Sort of ruined the idea of getting married in paradise for me."

"Then get married around here somewhere. Heck, you could get married at the courthouse, one of the local wineries, your grandmother's backyard—really, all the two of you need to do is pick a place, pick a date, and show up. And, of course, let me know where you're registered so I know what to buy you."

Was this her way of saying that she expected a wedding invitation? "You don't need to buy us anything."

"I'd like to." Her lips curled into a tentative smile. "That's what you do for an old friend, right?"

Were we friends again? Or was she referring to Steve?

I stifled a sigh, wishing I had gone for that patty melt when I had the chance.

"Sure," I said after a second of hesitation.

Heather's mouth immediately flat-lined as if she had read my mind, and I knew that I had to get out of there before I said something I'd regret.

"I should get going." I took one last sip before pushing off the sofa. "You have a kid to check on, and I have a dog to let out before he starts doing the potty dance."

I started toward the kitchen with my wineglass. "I'll just—"

"Don't worry about it," Heather said, taking it from me and placing our two glasses on the coffee table. Then, she wrapped her arms around me and gave me a vanilla-scented embrace that reminded me of the ice cream we churned the night of Brandy Langerfeld's slumber party.

That wretched sleepover that changed everything between us.

"Thanks again for everything you did," Heather murmured in my ear. "It meant a lot."

If I could have tapped out of this moment like a wrestler forfeiting a match, I would have. Because unlike last Saturday when she hugged me, Heather seemed determined to hold on until she broke down my defenses.

"It's good it's over." I pulled back, wanting this awkward feeling to also be over.

"Don't," she snapped.

I froze, feeling as stiff and geeky as the first time I danced with a boy. "Don't what?"

She released me with a sheepish grin. "I was gonna say don't make this weird. But something resembling normal might be asking for too much. At least for a while."

Might?

"No duh," I quipped, mimicking the eleven-year-old I was the last time I said those words to her.

Heather's grin widened. "Okay, fine. That was an understatement. Instead, how about this? Don't be a stranger."

I could live with that.

Chapter Thirty

When I stepped in from my garage ten minutes later, Fozzie wasn't at the door, wagging his tail with joy at the sight of me.

Of course, I had seen Steve's pickup parked outside before I pulled into my driveway, so I wasn't a bit surprised when I found my dog stuck like glue to his other favorite human. Especially since that human was on my couch eating out of one of the three white takeout boxes in front of him.

Steve paused the show he had been watching and waved his fork at me. "Where've you been?"

"You don't want to know," I groaned, slinging my tote over the back of a dining room chair. "What are you eating? I'm starving."

"You must've not seen my text that I was ordering Chinese."

I hung up my raincoat and offered him a smile of apology. "Sorry, I was out with my mother and then ran into an old friend." Sort of. "I guess I didn't hear the phone."

"I got enough for both of us, including that kung pao chicken you like."

And judging from the delicious aroma, I hoped to see some sweet and sour pork in one of those containers. "Awesome!"

Fozzie's tail wagged excitedly as I reached down to hug him around the ruff. "Hello, sweetheart. I'm so sorry I'm late getting home."

"Hello, my much better-smelling sweetheart," I said, dropping onto the couch to give Steve a kiss. "How was your day?"

"Long and a little crazy."

I could have used that same line to describe mine but decided not to go there. "Bummer, but at least it's over. I'm glad mine's over, too."

And my growling stomach was especially glad to see the takeout boxes waiting for me on my coffee table.

After I snuggled up next to him, Steve handed me the box of kung pao chicken while Fozzie sniffed the air with interest. "I saved you most of it."

"I guess you do love me."

"I was thinking of you," he said as I peeked into the remaining two boxes to see what else he had left for me.

A few meager wedges of pineapple drowning in sweet and sour sauce and a half container of fried rice. "But not enough to save me some pork."

"You snooze, you lose."

Steve leaned back, watching me as I forked a huge bite of lukewarm spicy chicken. "So, what exactly was going on tonight?"

I took the time to chew and swallow my food to think about how much I wanted to divulge. "My mother needed a ride to a business meeting with Veronica Lovely."

"A *business* meeting?" He smirked. "I take it your mother is still trying to get her to do that home improvement show."

"Still? She never stopped. And it seems that Veronica is just as interested in it as she is, assuming that they can find someone to be her partner on the show."

I didn't think there was any point in mentioning that Wyatt was the partner they both had in mind. Steve wouldn't be interested in the guy I had been so wrong about, and I didn't want to risk saying more than I should.

"Then what?" he asked. "You ran into a friend while you were there?"

I actually did. Crystal. But I had been stirring up such a concoction of lies and half-truths over the last few days that I couldn't stomach the idea of adding one more to the mix.

"No," I said, reaching for the rapidly cooling fried rice. "I stopped on my way home to see how Heather was doing."

I could feel his eyes on me and didn't want to see the obvious question I'd find waiting for me.

"Why?" he asked.

And there it was, whether I wanted to see it or not.

"Because I'm a nice person." Most of the time. "And because she's been having a hard time accepting that Kevin Lovely's death was entirely accidental."

"As I recall, she wasn't the only one."

I shrugged, focusing on the dog at my feet. "Only because I thought Heather had a point about the timing of the 911 calls."

"I can see how it looked from her perspective, so I'll give you that."

Forking another big bite of chicken, I prayed that he wouldn't ask any other probing questions.

Then, after a few seconds, he picked up the remote control from the coffee table and I thought I might be home-free.

He'd go back to watching his movie, and I'd be able to eat in peace.

"How's she doing?" Steve asked, toying with the remote.

So much for being home-free.

"You know Heather." Better than I did, given the history between the three of us. "I think she really liked the guy, but she'll be okay."

He nodded.

"I saw her new kitchen," I added. "It's beautiful."

"Yeah, I saw it when I was over there that night. Big improvement over the old, cracked tile she had before."

"I wouldn't know." And it chafed my hide a little that he did.

"And now that you make *house calls* to check in on her, you do." Steve's mouth quirked with amusement. "So, you two are friends again, huh? Go figure."

"I'm not exactly sure what we are." Whatever it was, it gave me sort of a settled feeling inside. Much like what the kung pao chicken was accomplishing. "But yeah. Go figure."

"Are you saying that I shouldn't expect to hear that you two are meeting for coffee next week?"

I set down the takeout box and fork so that I wouldn't chew my way through this entire conversation. "No, but I think she wants to come to our wedding."

His brow furrowing, Steve locked gazes with me. "She actually said that?"

"More hinted at it."

"She must not know that it could involve booking a flight to Hawaii."

"Actually, that's something I wanted to talk to you about." I smiled, my heart beating a happy rhythm as I took his hand. "Because I was thinking about how much easier it would be on everyone if we got married somewhere around here. Especially with Donna being pregnant."

His lips curled. "I'm sure they'd agree, but the most important thing in all this is what *you* want."

"What *we* want," I said, correcting him.

"Okay. What do we want?"

"We need to talk about that. But probably a simple ceremony somewhere nearby."

He nodded. "Simple is good. This doesn't have to be overly complicated. Just pick a place, tell me when to show up, and I'll be there."

"That's almost word for word what one of my friends said."

"Smart friend. Maybe she can help you find a venue."

There was absolutely no way I was going to ask his old girlfriend to help me plan my wedding.

I leaned my head against his shoulder, reveling in his warmth. "I'd rather have you help me do that."

"No problem," Steve said. "When?"

"If you have time this weekend, we could drive out to a few places. I saw a lot of them last year with my mother, but you haven't."

He let out a breathy laugh. "We can do that, but I meant when do you want to get married?"

I turned to look into his eyes. "As soon as possible."

"Good answer."

Then he kissed me.

THE END

ABOUT THE AUTHOR

Wendy Delaney writes fun-filled cozy mysteries and is the award-winning author of the Working Stiffs Mystery series. A long-time member of Mystery Writers of America, she's a Food Network addict and pastry chef wannabe. When she's not killing off story people she can be found on her treadmill, working off the calories from her latest culinary adventure.

Originally from the Pacific Northwest, Wendy now lives in the Hill Country of Texas with the love of her life and is a proud grandma.

How best to connect: For book news please visit her website at www.wendydelaney.com, email her at wendy@wendydelaney.com, and follow her on Facebook at www.facebook.com/wendy.delaney.908.

www.ingramcontent.com/pod-product-compliance
Lightning Source LLC
Chambersburg PA
CBHW030237200626
46816CB00002BA/402